FOR BETTER OR FOR WORSE

"We're going to be trying an experiment this year. It's a social studies project that's had interesting results in several schools in other parts of the state, and I think it's time for Fenton Hall to give it a try. . . . It's called Junior Family Week," Miss Fenton announced. "It's a role-playing project where you will all act the part of responsible married adults for the next five days."

"Married?" someone yelped from a couple of rows behind Stevie. "My parents won't even let me date yet!"

"All right, all right," Miss Fenton called, raising her hands for order. "Now let me tell you how the project will work. You'll be divided into couples, and each couple will be expected to complete a variety of exercises designed to teach a range of life skills."

Stevie wrinkled her nose at that, thinking that Junior Family Week sounded pretty goofy so far. *What kind of "life skills" does it take to be married?* she thought. *I mean, fall in love, tie the knot, move in together, take turns cooking dinner. Big fat whopping deal.*

Don't miss any of the excitement
at PINE HOLLOW,
where friends come first:

PINE HOLLOW®

BACK IN THE SADDLE

BY BONNIE BRYANT

BANTAM BOOKS
NEW YORK • TORONTO • LONDON • SYDNEY • AUCKLAND

*My special thanks to Catherine Hapka for her help
in the writing of this book.*

Special thanks to Laura Roper of Sir "B" Farms

RL: 5.0, AGES 012 AND UP

BACK IN THE SADDLE
A Bantam Book/June 2000

ISBN: 0-553-49302-7

Visit us on the Web! www.randomhouse.com
Educators and librarians, for a variety of teaching tools, visit us at
www.randomhouse.com/teachers

Published simultaneously in the United States and Canada

Bantam Books is an imprint of Random House Children's Books.
BANTAM BOOKS and the rooster colophon are registered trademarks of
Random House, Inc. Bantam Books, 1540 Broadway, New York, New York
10036

PRINTED IN THE UNITED STATES OF AMERICA

OPM   10 9 8 7 6 5 4 3 2 1

ONE
1

"Thanks for the ride, Stevie," Scott Forester said as he undid his seat belt and crawled out of the backseat of the small two-door car, tilting his broad shoulders sideways to squeeze through the narrow opening.

Alex Lake climbed out after him. "After riding with Stevie, I bet you can't wait till your own car's back from the shop, huh?" he joked, slapping Scott on the shoulder.

Scott laughed and pretended to shudder. "Well, I wasn't going to say anything, but . . ."

Stevie Lake rolled her eyes as her twin brother and their friend jogged toward the front steps of Fenton Hall, the private high school they all attended. Then she turned to Callie Forester, Scott's sister, who had gotten out on the passenger's side and was waiting by the car. "So," Stevie said, glancing up at the grand old school building towering above the student parking lot. "I guess this means Thanksgiving break's really over, huh?"

Callie yawned and tossed her long, straight blond hair over her shoulder. Then she picked up the smooth wooden cane that was leaning against the car's battered blue fender. "Guess so," she agreed. "Ready to head in?"

Stevie nodded, slightly distracted from the conversation by the sight of that cane. It had been about six months since the car accident that had left Callie unable to walk on her own. Many, many hours of hard work and determination had helped her regain control over her body, and a week ago she had finally been able to shed the metal crutches she hated so much.

"Just a sec." Stevie leaned down to retrieve her trigonometry notebook from inside the car. "By the way, I have to tell you, you totally amaze me. I can't believe you're walking so well already."

"Thanks." Callie sounded pleased. "I didn't use my crutches at all last week while we were away. I've hardly had to use this cane, either, though Mom and Dad insist I carry it around in case I get tired." She slung the handle of the cane through the strap of her backpack and then pulled the pack onto one shoulder. "And now that I've got this independent walking thing down, I can't wait to get back into training again. I want to start right away. As in, like, today. I called Max yesterday afternoon as soon as we got home from the airport to make sure Barq would be available."

Stevie nodded, guessing from the satisfied expression on Callie's face that Max Regnery, the owner of Pine Hollow Stables, had agreed to let her ride the horse she wanted. "That's great," Stevie said sincerely. Callie was a pretty private person a lot of the time, and she hadn't said much to her friends about just how hard the past few months had been on her. In some ways, Stevie suspected that not being able to ride as well as she once had must have been even harder on Callie than not being able to walk without crutches. Even though Callie had done a lot of therapeutic riding as part of her physical therapy, Stevie knew that walking and trotting around the indoor ring at Pine Hollow couldn't really compare to training for and competing in endurance races. Callie had been a junior endurance champion before moving to Willow Creek, Virginia, the previous June. "Barq will be a great horse to get you back into the swing of things," Stevie commented. "And maybe soon you'll be ready to start looking for your own competition horse again."

Callie nodded but didn't respond, which Stevie took as a cue to change the subject. A horse Callie had been interested in buying was killed in the same accident that had injured her, and Stevie certainly didn't want to bring up those memories again. "Come on," she said eagerly. "Let's practice that new independent walking of yours and get inside."

Callie shot her a surprised and slightly suspicious

look. "What are you sounding so chipper about? This is school, remember? And last I heard, school wasn't exactly your favorite place to be. Especially on Monday mornings. And even more especially on Monday mornings after weeklong vacations."

Stevie grinned. "I almost forgot, you weren't around this past week," she said. "You don't know about my fabulous new career as an internationally renowned journalist."

"Huh?" Callie looked confused.

Stevie started walking toward the school as she explained. "Well, like Alex and I were saying in the car on the way here, Mom and Dad finally ended our grounding last weekend, right after Thanksgiving break started."

Callie nodded. "I just wish Scott and I had been around to help you guys celebrate."

"I know." Stevie shrugged. "Believe me, I was wishing that too all last week when I was forced to actually hang out with my brother at Pine Hollow for lack of anything more interesting to do."

She paused for a moment, feeling a twinge of guilt. The last thing she wanted to do was sound ungrateful for the fact that her parents had finally let her and Alex off the hook for drinking at a party back in October. But it really had been kind of disappointing to suddenly be free and to realize that none of their friends was around to help them appreciate it. One of Stevie's longtime best friends, Carole Han-

4

son, had been grounded herself for cheating on a test. Her other best friend, Lisa Atwood, had been in California visiting her father, stepmother, and half sister. Stevie's boyfriend, Phil Marsten, had been home in bed all week fighting off a mild case of pneumonia. And finally, Callie and Scott had been visiting their old hometown on the West Coast, partly to see old friends, but mostly so that their congressman father could keep in touch with his constituents.

"Anyway," Stevie continued as she and Callie walked slowly across the fractured pavement of the parking lot, heading for Fenton Hall's broad stone steps. "The point is, I guess I was a little bored. It was great to hang out at Pine Hollow again, to spend time riding Belle and just be free, you know? But I missed having all you guys around." She shrugged. "So when I found out that Deborah was working on a story about retired show horses, I was totally psyched to help her out."

"A newspaper story, you mean?" Callie looked interested. "What was the article about?"

Stevie smiled. "I'm just getting to that." Deborah Hale, Max Regnery's wife, was a reporter for a major Washington, D.C., daily. She and Max had met and married several years earlier, soon after Deborah had come to Pine Hollow to do some background research for her first horse-related story. Since then, she had written several other equine articles, though she also reported on a wide variety of other topics, from politics to social issues to the environment. "The story didn't sound too thrilling at first, actually," Stevie admitted. "It was just supposed to be a nice little article about an old lady who takes care of old horses. But then we got out there and realized there was a lot more to it than that."

She quickly filled Callie in on the rest of the details. At first, when she and Deborah had arrived at the retirement farm, everything had seemed fine. The place was clean, the woman running it was friendly, and the horses looked healthy—from a distance. When Stevie got closer to one of the retirees, though, she'd noticed some subtle health problems that made her suspicious. After that Deborah had taken over, digging out all the details of the real story: The woman was cutting corners on the horses' care to make more money. Deborah had launched a full investigation, and the resulting story had run in the previous Friday's issue of the newspaper.

When Stevie finished, Callie looked suitably impressed. "Wow," she said as the two of them started up the school steps toward the heavy wooden front doors. "Sounds like Deborah was lucky you were there and paying attention."

"I guess she was," Stevie agreed, not bothering with false modesty. She was proud of herself for the part she'd played in helping those horses, and she didn't care who knew it. "But I was pretty lucky, too. See, Deborah let me help her out a little with the writing, and she talked her editor into mentioning me in the byline. That was totally cool. So I figured, hey, why not try to recapture the feeling?"

Callie nodded thoughtfully. "So you're going to join the school paper?"

Stevie grinned. "You're a genius, Forester," she said. "And you're exactly right. The *Sentinel* needs me. I mean, what other Fenton Hall student has actually been published in the Washington *Reporter*?"

"Probably none," Callie agreed with a smile.

Stevie took the last few steps two at a time and then held the door open for Callie, who was following more slowly. When they were both inside, Stevie checked her watch. She still had plenty of time before she had to be in homeroom. "I'd better get up to the media room."

"Okay. Good luck." Callie waved and hoisted her backpack a little higher on her shoulder. "See you at lunch, if you're not busy tracking down breaking news or something."

The two of them parted ways. Stevie headed straight for the south stairwell, which would lead her up to the school's media room on the third floor. She was so busy making a mental list of all the brilliant story ideas she'd come up with over the past few days that she wasn't paying much attention to where she was going. As she rounded the corner into the stairwell at a swift trot, she almost crashed into a tall, slender, attractive girl with long dark hair.

Stevie pulled herself up just in time. "Whoa! Sorry!" she exclaimed breathlessly before she'd even had a chance to recognize the other girl. Then she frowned. "Oh. Veronica. It's just you."

Veronica diAngelo gave Stevie an annoyed glare. Glancing down at her suede jacket, she brushed an invisible spot of lint off the lapel. "Stevie Lake," she said in the slow, haughty, deliberate tone she saved for anyone she thought was beneath her, which was just about everyone. "Doing your best ladylike impression of a freight train again, I see?"

Stevie rolled her eyes. *Yeah, right*, she thought. *Like Veronica has ever actually* seen *a freight train. Stretch limo is more her speed.*

But she didn't bother to respond out loud. Back in junior high, when Veronica had been taking riding lessons at Pine Hollow, the two girls had been at each other's throats almost constantly. Veronica's snobby, superior attitude always rubbed Stevie the wrong way, while Stevie's rambunctious, fun-loving nature had often clashed with Veronica's sense of self-importance. In the past few years, however, Veronica had turned her attention from expensive horses to rich guys. She and Stevie had separate groups of friends, and it was pretty easy for them to ignore each other most of the time. And Stevie had to admit that their truce— intentional or not—made her life a lot easier.

8

"Whatever," Stevie told Veronica shortly. "Now, if you'll excuse me, I have something important to do."

"I'm so sure." Veronica rolled her eyes with a slightly bemused expression that indicated exactly how important she thought anything Stevie had to do could be. As she turned, though, she paused and glanced at Stevie again. "By the way," she said, "I hear Nicole Adams is taking up riding again. And that your very own twin brother has been playing the happy little tour guide for the past week. I guess it's true what they say: When the cat's away . . ." She let her voice trail off suggestively, then smirked and hurried out of the stairwell before Stevie could come up with a suitable reply.

Gritting her teeth—why did Veronica still have the ability to get to her, even now?—Stevie headed up the stairs. She knew exactly where Veronica was going with her stupid little remark. Up until a year ago, Stevie never would have guessed that her twin brother and one of her best friends would fall in love. But Alex and Lisa had been a couple for the better part of a year now. They'd had a few rocky patches in their relationship lately, but Stevie was really starting to believe that they were meant to be together forever, just like her and Phil. When Lisa had left for California the weekend before Thanksgiving, Alex had spent the first day or two moping around and bemoaning her absence. Then he'd run into Nicole Adams at the stable.

Poor Alex, Stevie thought, her mind flashing to the image of her brother gazing at Nicole's bouncy blond hair and amazing figure. *What does he know about dealing with a total flirt like Nicole? He was just being friendly.* Even though she'd discovered that Nicole had been a rider at Pine Hollow way before Stevie had started taking lessons there, she wasn't convinced that the other girl's sudden resurgence of interest in horses was the only reason for her return. Stevie still remembered how her drunken brother had slow-danced with Nicole at their party after a huge fight with Lisa. *I'm sure Veronica remembers that, too,* she thought grimly. *And I'm sure she's totally grooving on the idea that Nicole might be causing trouble between Alex and Lisa. Not that there's really any chance of that. Now that Lisa's back, everything will be fine.*

Stevie banished Lisa, Alex, Nicole, and especially Veronica diAngelo from her mind as she approached the media room. The glass-paneled door was propped open with a large dictionary, and classical music was playing softly from somewhere inside. Stepping over the threshold, Stevie cast a curious eye around the spacious, window-lined room. She'd been there many times before, usually to drop off a student government announcement for the paper or to check out a tape from the extensive video library. But for the first time, she really took it all in. The media room had been created by knocking down the walls between two rooms, allowing enough space for the newspaper

10

and yearbook staffs to work, as well as plenty of storage for the bulky audiovisual equipment that wouldn't fit into the cramped, dungeonlike library on the ground floor. Unlike most of the classrooms at Fenton Hall, which echoed the building's old-fashioned exterior with their arched windows and scuffed wooden floors, the media room had a modern look. Metal shelves stretched along two of the walls, holding hundreds of video- and audiotapes, CD-ROMs, and miscellaneous pieces of computer equipment. A separate shelving unit against a third wall provided a home for a few TV sets, a couple of hand-held video cameras, and an old-fashioned film projector, as well as the portable stereo that was the source of the classical music. The floor had been covered with sisal carpeting, and long, low-slung tables were scattered here and there, along with a few armchairs. There was even an old, slightly battle-scarred couch resting beneath one broad window. At the moment the place was almost empty, with just a couple of students bent over their work in different parts of the room. Still, Stevie was sure that by Thursday morning the place would be bustling as the entire staff worked to meet their deadline and pull the paper together in time to print it.

Wow, Stevie thought, a slow smile spreading across her face. *So this is where I'm going to be spending my time from now on. Not too shabby.*

Just then a girl sitting at a computer near the window glanced up from her keyboard and spotted her. "Hello?" she called. "Can I help you?"

"Hi! I was looking for the editor," Stevie replied, vaguely recognizing the other girl as a freshman named Mary or Marnie or something like that. "Is she around?"

"She just ran to the bathroom," the freshman replied. "Should be back soon."

Stevie nodded her thanks, then wandered toward the long wall opposite the door. Framed past issues of the *Sentinel* decorated the spaces between the windows, and as Stevie looked them over, she felt more and more excited about her plans.

Wow, she thought, walking slowly down the length of the wall and scanning each framed page. *I guess this is one of those "advantages" Mom and Dad are always talking about when they tell people why they decided to send us to private school.*

Over the years, Stevie had occasionally wished that her parents had decided to send her to Willow Creek High, the public school across town, where she could be with her best friends all day long. But at that moment, she really did feel incredibly lucky to be at Fenton Hall. She knew that Lisa had briefly joined her school paper during her sophomore year, but she'd quit in frustration after just a couple of months. Although the middle school managed to put out a respectable paper, Willow Creek High's *Crier* was published sporadically at best, and the previous year the three student editors had spent more time juggling for power than they had in doing any actual work. The result was a dull, error-riddled publication that rarely filled more than eight pages, and which most of the student body ignored unless they were making it into spitballs.

By contrast, the *Sentinel* came out every Friday morning without fail, had won numerous local awards, and had even been a finalist in the state journalism competition the previous year. The current editor, a senior named Theresa Cruz, was continuing the tradition of lively and varied reporting on all sorts of topics, from the smallest student concerns to serious national controversies. Like most Fenton Hall students, Stevie never took her seat in homeroom on Friday morning without first grabbing a copy of that week's *Sentinel* from the basket near the door.

Stevie was reading an article from the previous spring about the public school board's proposal to institute a school uniform when she heard the girl at the computer speak again. "Hey, Theresa," the freshman called. "Someone's here to see you."

Stevie spun around and saw that a short, pretty, olive-skinned girl with large, serious dark eyes and close-cropped black hair had just entered the room. "Hi, Theresa!" Stevie exclaimed, hurrying toward the older girl. "I'm Stevie Lake."

Theresa Cruz nodded, a slight smile brightening

her serious face. "Yes, I know who you are," she said. "What can I do for you, Stevie?"

Stevie grinned, wondering if Theresa had seen her byline in the *Reporter* the previous week. Then she realized that Theresa probably knew her from before that. For one thing, reporters from the *Sentinel* had interviewed Stevie several times just a month earlier. She had been Scott's campaign manager when he'd won the office of student body president. Besides that, Stevie had never exactly been shy, and Fenton Hall was a relatively small school. She knew just about everyone, and just about everyone knew her.

In any case, Stevie decided there was no point in beating around the bush. "I'm here to join the *Sentinel*," she explained. "I want to be a reporter."

Theresa didn't bat an eye. "Okay, great," she said calmly, taking a seat at the nearest empty table. "We're always glad to have newbies. Why don't you come back at lunchtime and we can talk more about what you and the *Sentinel* have to offer each other?"

"Sure thing," Stevie agreed. She was a little disappointed at being put off, but she figured it was for the best. At lunchtime, she and Theresa would have much more time to talk. That way they could figure out which beat would be best for Stevie—politics? sports? student life?—and figure out how soon she could get her first story into print. *And then my spectacular new career can really get off the ground,* she thought with a grin as she glanced around the media room once more before heading for the door. *I can't wait!*

A little later that morning, Carole Hanson was standing in front of her open locker, staring at a photograph she'd taped to the inside of the metal door. It was a picture of her horse, Starlight, standing in the back paddock at Pine Hollow and looking over the fence. As she gazed into his big, dark eyes, she could swear she heard him speaking.

Carole, he said woefully, in a voice that sounded an awful lot like Mr. Ed's, *why don't you ever come to Pine Hollow and ride me anymore?*

"Carole!" a much more familiar voice said from right behind her.

Carole jumped, then turned with an embarrassed laugh. "Lisa," she said. "Hi. Uh, you startled me."

"Sorry." Lisa Atwood smiled, her gaze straying to the photo. "I didn't mean to interrupt your mental conversation with Starlight."

Carole blushed. Her friends knew her too well. Then again, almost everyone who'd ever met Carole knew that she spent much more time thinking about horses than about anything else. Carole knew that some people thought she was a little strange—a bit too single-minded in her devotion to horses. Then again, she thought anyone who didn't have any interest in horses or riding was pretty strange. What did *those* people find to think about all day long? She couldn't imagine.

Carole had known for as long as she could remember that she planned to spend her life working full-time with her favorite creatures. The only question remaining was what, exactly, she was going to do. Would she find her future in riding horses in competition? Training them? Healing them? Or maybe following in Max's footsteps and teaching others to love them as much as she did? Carole wasn't sure yet which path was meant for her, but she was determined to figure it out soon.

"So what's up?" she asked Lisa, quickly grabbing her English notebook and slamming her locker door shut.

Lisa checked her watch. "We have a substitute in senior lit this week, so I have a study hall next period. I figured it was the perfect chance to track you down and catch up." She smiled, pushing a strand of blond hair out of her eyes. "I miss you, you know, and I figured you missed me a little, too. Almost as much as Starlight, maybe."

Carole laughed. "Definitely," she teased. "Definitely *almost* as much, I mean. Come on, why don't you walk me to my English class?" She smiled ruefully. "These days, I can't afford to be late to anything. Otherwise Dad might not let me ride until Memorial Day."

The two girls fell into step as they headed down

the crowded hall. Carole was glad Lisa had found her. One of the hardest things about being grounded was being kept away from horses. But being kept from her friends was hard, too. Stevie and Lisa had been there for all of the important moments in her life, good and bad, for so long that Carole could hardly remember a time when she hadn't known them. Her life just didn't seem quite complete when she couldn't talk to them about things. The three of them had always complemented each other perfectly, their friendship stronger because of their differences rather than in spite of them. Fun-loving, impulsive Stevie was the group's clown, but she also offered strength and loyalty that were second to none. Lisa was the most logical and sensible of the trio, a responsible citizen and an A student. Of course, that didn't stop her from occasionally succumbing to doubts or insecurity, especially since her parents' divorce. Carole sometimes thought of herself as the glue that cemented their three-way friendship. Her friends' strong opinions rarely clashed, but when they did, Carole was always there to remind them that their friendship was more important than any disagreement.

Sometimes Carole missed the days when the three of them would spend virtually all their time together, not seeming to want or need anyone else. That didn't mean that Carole didn't like Callie and Scott or Phil and Alex. It just sometimes seemed that there were so many other people in her friends' lives these days that there wasn't enough time left for their friendship.

"So how was your trip?" Carole asked, dragging her mind out of the past. She seemed to spend too much time there lately, especially considering that she was trying her best to focus on the future. "Did your father give you a hard time about the college thing?" While Carole and Stevie were juniors who had done little to prepare for college so far, aside from taking the PSATs a month or so earlier, Lisa was a senior, and she'd recently decided to attend nearby Northern Virginia University. Unfortunately, she hadn't shared her decision with either of her parents until after she'd already responded to the school, and Carole knew that they were very upset about that, especially since Lisa had applied to several much more prestigious schools in other parts of the country.

Lisa wrinkled her nose. "Yeah, he was all over me at first," she said. "But he got distracted when my brother turned up."

"Your brother?" Carole was surprised. Lisa's older brother, Peter, had been living abroad for so long that Carole had met him only a few times. She raised her voice as they turned a corner and entered a different hallway, where half a dozen guys were horsing around. "I didn't know he was coming back to the States for Thanksgiving."

"None of us did," Lisa replied, dodging as a foam football whizzed past her head. "But that wasn't the biggest surprise. It turns out he went and got married without telling any of us. Plus, his new wife's a few years older than him, recently divorced with a couple of kids."

Carole shook her head, her eyes widening. "Wow. Talk about a bombshell."

"I know." Lisa sighed. "But I'll fill you in on all that later when we have more time to talk. Right now, the major news flash is that Rafe dumped Mom while I was away."

"Really?" Carole said, not certain how she should respond. Lisa's mother had been dating a much younger man named Rafe for a while now—Carole had lost track of how long. But she knew that Lisa had never liked him. So why did she actually seem upset that he was out of her mother's life?

"Uh-huh. She took it kind of hard." Lisa bit her lip, casting her eyes downward as she walked, a slight frown creasing her forehead. "She's pretty bummed."

"Oh." Now Carole understood. After the breakup of her twenty-seven-year marriage, Mrs. Atwood had been deeply depressed for a very long time. Inappropriate or not, her relationship with Rafe had snapped her out of her gloom and made her start living life again.

"It's not like I miss having Rafe around or anything, but I really wish Mom had dumped him instead of the other way around," Lisa commented, pausing and bending over to smooth out one of her leggings, which was slightly bunched above the top of her left ankle boot.

"Hey, Atwood! Looking good, sweet thang." A popular senior named Nate Mondale grinned and winked at Lisa as he loped past into a nearby classroom.

The only indication that Lisa had heard the comment was a slight pink flush that colored her high cheekbones as she straightened up. Carole had always known that her friend was beautiful—she'd had guys asking her out for as long as Carole had known her. Even her long-term relationship with Alex didn't stop guys like Nate from lusting after her.

I guess that's another way the three of us are different, Carole thought, not for the first time. She glanced at her friend out of the corner of her eye. *Lisa's always been a man magnet, with guys falling all over themselves to be with her. Stevie's always been kind of a tomboy, so lots of guys have liked her, too. But Stevie went out and found the perfect guy for her, and they're practically an old married couple by now. Lisa and Alex hooked up, and they've been living happily ever after. And then there's me: Ms. Pathetic.*

For about the millionth time in the past couple of weeks, she thought about Ben Marlow. She'd known Ben for more than a year and a half, ever since he'd started working as a stable hand at Pine Hollow. But even after all that time, she still had no idea what she thought of him. Or what she felt about him. The

20

only thing she knew for sure was that she felt *some-thing*. But was it merely friendship born of their mutual love of horses, of admiration and respect for Ben's immense talent in communicating with his favorite animals? Or could there be something more between them?

For a long time, Carole hadn't really thought much about it. She'd never been that comfortable when it came to dating and romance, and it had seemed easier just to accept that she and Ben were friends and coworkers without worrying about the strange feelings she sometimes had when she saw him.

Then Ben had kissed her and everything had changed. Now she couldn't look at him or even think about him without blushing and feeling uncomfortable, especially since Ben himself seemed determined to pretend that it had never happened. To make matters even more complicated, Carole had recently discovered that Ben was somehow related to an intriguing little girl with huge, dark eyes. But little Zani seemed to be one more topic that Ben wasn't interested in discussing with Carole. So she still had no more idea of who the four-year-old child was than she knew what Ben really thought of her. . . .

Glancing over at Lisa to see if she'd noticed her consternation, Carole saw that her friend was looking anxious, probably still thinking about her mother. That seemed to be Carole's cue to change the subject—for both their sakes. The first new topic that sprang to mind was one that was never far from Carole's heart. "Have you been to Pine Hollow since you got back?" she asked as they reached the door to Carole's classroom.

Lisa nodded. "Alex and I met there yesterday for a ride," she said. "Stevie was there, too." She shot Carole a quick glance. "But it just wasn't the same without you."

"Thanks." Carole shrugged and sighed. "You know, I feel like it's been forever since I was there. I still can't believe how much longer I have to stay away." Not wanting her friend to think she was complaining—after all, she'd brought this punishment on herself by cheating on that test—she cleared her throat. "Um, but I'm trying to look on the bright side," she said. "I figure since I can't ride for a while, at least I can spend the time being, you know, constructive. I want to try to figure out what I really want to do with my life. You know, specifically."

"Really?" Lisa looked surprised. "Hey, good for you. So have you narrowed it down yet?"

"No," Carole admitted. "I'm trying, but I'm not quite sure how to go about it. The only thing I'm sure about is that I'm seventeen years old now, and it's definitely time to get a clue."

Lisa nodded thoughtfully. "I know what you mean. Maybe you could start by listing all the careers you can think of," she suggested.

"That's mostly what I've been doing so far."

"Good," Lisa said. "When you have the whole list of possibilities, you can figure out the pros and cons of each one. That way you can maybe start to eliminate some of the ones with way more cons and think more seriously about the ones that are mostly pros." She shrugged. "That's basically how I did it when I decided where to go to college. When I decided the pros of NVU were totally overwhelming, my mind was made up."

Carole couldn't help thinking that deciding her entire future sounded like a huge and daunting task, no matter how organized she was about it. But before she could figure out how to express that to Lisa, the bell rang, signaling that third period was about to begin. "Oops," she said. "Better go. See you later." Pushing the future out of her head—for the moment, at least—she hurried into her classroom.

TWO

"And of course, one always has a responsibility to one's sources," Theresa said somberly.

Stevie nodded, wondering if the editor could hear her stomach grumbling. She'd hurried straight to their meeting from her fourth-period class, not even bothering to stop at her locker and pick up her bag lunch. It was rapidly becoming clear that that had been a big mistake. Theresa had been droning on and on about journalistic ethics for almost five minutes straight, and Stevie had hardly been able to get a word in edgewise.

"Okay," she broke in as Theresa paused for breath. "I get it. Following the rules is key. But what about the good stuff? As in the writing and reporting of actual stories? Isn't that kind of the point of the whole deal?"

Theresa blinked. "Well, yes," she allowed. "But there's a lot more that goes into a good newspaper than just what gets printed on the page. If all *The Wall Street Journal* paid attention to was writing and reporting, it wouldn't be the great publication it is. And a good newspaperman or -woman should be familiar with all aspects of the news business, from financing to circulation to how the ink gets into the presses."

"Right," Stevie said, her voice firmer this time. "That's all, like, really interesting and everything. And maybe we can talk about it some more later. I'd love to learn all about the news biz. But for now, I really want to move on to what I can do for the *Sentinel.* As in, how to get started."

"Of course," Theresa said. "I was just getting to that. I thought you could start right away—"

"Great!" Stevie interrupted eagerly.

Theresa nodded. "Yes, I'd love for you to jump right in and assist with proofreading this week's issue, and we can always use help with distribution once the papers are printed. Do you have a way to get to school early on Friday? Say, around six-thirty?"

Stevie blinked. "Huh? Um, maybe I wasn't that clear before," she said. "But when I said I wanted to join the paper, I meant I wanted to *write* for the paper. Not proofread and do that other stuff."

"I realize that. But every good journalist has to pay his or her dues," Theresa said, her gaze slightly reproachful. "Besides, proofreading and distribution are vitally important jobs. If they don't get done, there's no paper. At least no paper worth reading."

Stevie had to stop herself from rolling her eyes.

Distribution and proofreading might be "vitally important," but they also sounded vitally boring. Still, she didn't want to alienate her new editor by saying so. "All right," she said appeasingly. "Um, I'm sure I could squeeze in some distribution time before school on Friday or whatever. But can't I do some writing at the same time? How am I going to get any useful experience if you don't even give me a shot?"

Theresa shrugged. "You make a valid point, Stevie. I suppose in a week or two, if all goes well, we could meet again and talk about your taking over a couple of small writing tasks, just to see how you do."

Stevie started to smile. *Finally!* she thought. *Now we're getting somewhere.*

Theresa rubbed her cheek thoughtfully. "I suppose we could let you try writing out the weekly lunch menus. Or maybe you could edit the classified ads— you know, call the numbers to make sure they're legit, check the wording and spelling, that sort of thing."

Stevie's smile faded quickly. But before she could say anything, she was interrupted by the loud, staticky crackle of the PA speaker over the door. "Attention!" the tinny voice of their headmistress, Miss Fenton, announced. "Attention, students. I would like all juniors to finish their lunches quickly and come to the auditorium for a special assembly. That's juniors only, please. To the auditorium immediately. Thank you for your cooperation."

"I guess I'd better go," Stevie told Theresa, a little relieved to have their meeting cut short.

So much for my high-flying career as a star reporter, she thought grimly as she stood and grabbed her backpack. *Thanks to Theresa, it's totally stalling on the runway. Still, maybe this assembly will give me a chance to come up with a plan to convince her what a waste it will be if all I get to do for the next six months is hunch over somebody else's breaking news story with a dictionary and a grammar handbook.*

As she hurried down the empty third-floor hallway toward the stairs, Stevie wondered what the sudden assembly was all about. It wasn't like Miss Fenton to be so mysterious.

It's for juniors only, she reminded herself as she rounded the corner into the stairwell. *That means it's probably got something to do with the PSATs or something like that. Miss Fenton probably wants to call us together to announce that Sue Berry got the highest score in the history of the world, or maybe to humiliate us all by reading off our scores in front of the whole class.*

She was only kidding about that last part. The scores for the standardized college-entrance prep test that all juniors had taken earlier that fall would be sent directly to their homes. In fact, now that Stevie thought about it, they were probably due to arrive any day now.

Oh, well, Stevie thought. *I just hope Alex and I did respectably enough that Mom and Dad won't ground us all over again.* Taking the last three steps in one jump, she scooted around the corner on the second-floor landing and started down the next flight.

The auditorium was on the first floor, just down the hall from the school cafeteria, so Stevie was one of the last to arrive. As she paused in the wide, arched entrance, glancing around for a free seat, she spotted Callie waving to her from near the front of the large, cavernous room.

As Stevie hurried toward her friend, she was so distracted by thinking about her meeting with Theresa that it took her a moment or two to recognize the slightly desperate expression on Callie's face. Then she noticed the pudgy, moon-faced guy sitting next to her.

Yikes, she thought. *Looks like George has Callie cornered again. No wonder she's making like a windmill to get me over there.*

Stevie was happy to come to her friend's rescue if she could, even though she still didn't quite get why Callie wouldn't just tell George to get lost. It wasn't as though Callie had trouble speaking her mind. At first Stevie had thought there might be a chance that the mismatched pair would hit it off—both were smart, both were excellent riders. And despite the slender, cool good looks that guaranteed Callie the attention of just about any guy she wanted, she had already proved herself willing to risk gossip and ridicule by going to a school dance with the short, dumpy, unpopular George. But after that one evening, Callie had decided that the two of them should just be friends. So why didn't George seem to be getting the hint?

Stevie didn't worry about that for long. As she reached the row where Callie and George were sitting, she saw that Alex was sitting in the row right behind them with a few of his soccer teammates. "Glad you could make it, sis," he greeted her, smacking the back of the empty seat beside Callie. "We saved you a seat."

"Thanks." Stevie slid into the seat just as Miss Fenton strode out onto the creaky wooden stage and clapped her hands for attention.

"Thank you for your quick response, students," the headmistress said in her reedy voice. "I'm sure you'll be as excited as I am when you hear why I've gathered you all together."

"Early graduation?" Alex whispered loudly, making his soccer friends snort with laughter. Stevie sank down in her seat to hide her own grin.

Miss Fenton shot a sharp glance their way, then continued. "We're going to be trying an experiment this year. It's a social studies project that's had interesting results in several schools in other parts of the state, and I think it's time for Fenton Hall to give it a try."

Stevie exchanged curious glances with Callie. What kind of project was Miss Fenton talking about?

All around them, other students were murmuring to each other, obviously wondering the same thing.

The headmistress didn't keep them in suspense. "It's called Junior Family Week," she announced. "It's a role-playing project where you will all act the part of responsible married adults for the next five days."

"Married?" someone yelped from a couple of rows behind Stevie. "My parents won't even let me date yet!"

The entire auditorium erupted in laughter. Even Miss Fenton smiled. Meanwhile, Stevie craned her neck to catch a glimpse of the girl who'd called out. "I bet that was Lorraine Olsen," she told Callie with a grin. "She's always complaining about not being able to date. But actually, her folks just won't let her go anywhere with a guy in a car. She could go on three dates in one day, as long as she was willing to walk."

Callie smiled briefly, but Stevie couldn't help noticing that she seemed distracted. With a shrug, Stevie returned her attention to the stage.

"All right, all right," Miss Fenton called, raising her hands for order. Finally, when everyone had settled down, she continued. "Now, let me tell you how the project will work. You'll be divided into couples, and each couple will be expected to complete a variety of exercises designed to teach a range of life skills."

Stevie wrinkled her nose at that, thinking that

Junior Family Week sounded pretty goofy so far. *What kind of "life skills" does it take to be married?* she thought. *I mean, fall in love, tie the knot, move in together, take turns cooking dinner. Big fat whopping deal.*

"The project will begin this afternoon," Miss Fenton went on. "Instead of going to your regular seventh-period classes, you should all return here to the auditorium for our first Family Week meeting. For the remainder of the week, the meetings will take place during a different class period each day."

"All right!" Alex exclaimed. "No seventh period? That means no trig quiz this week. I'm loving this marriage project already!"

Stevie couldn't help agreeing with her twin on that one. "A period off from regular classes every day?" she whispered to Callie gleefully. "Cool deal! I just wish Phil went to school here. It'd be kind of fun to play house with him." She grinned wickedly.

Once again, Callie forced herself to smile back. But her mind really wasn't on Stevie and her boyfriend. Instead, she was very aware of George's arm lying casually on the armrest just inches from her body. She kept her gaze straight ahead, focused on the stage, but she could almost feel George glancing her way every two seconds. Why hadn't she tried harder to avoid sitting with him in this assembly?

Miss Fenton was still talking, explaining that several expert speakers would be coming to the school over the course of the week to talk to them about different aspects of marriage and family life. She also listed some of the assignments they would have to complete, from making choices about jobs and children to making a household budget.

But Callie wasn't really paying attention. She was too busy dreading the next few minutes. She could picture it now—knowing George, he would probably be down on one knee as soon as Miss Fenton gave the word to divide into couples, begging for her hand in fake marriage. *Of course, that's only if we get to pick our own partners,* Callie thought, a spark of hope flaring in her mind. *And how likely is that? The last thing Miss Fenton would want is a bunch of real-life couples feeling like they had permission to "play house," as Stevie put it.*

Someone raised a hand from near the back of the auditorium. "Yes, Veronica?" Miss Fenton said, pointing. "Do you have a question?"

"Yes, Miss Fenton," Veronica diAngelo replied. "Are we going to get a grade for this project?"

"Figures that would be her first question," Stevie murmured with a grimace. "All she cares about is what's in it for her."

Callie shrugged. She wasn't crazy about Veronica, but she had to admit that she admired the other girl's directness and self-confidence. "I wonder how they're going to choose our partners?" she whispered to

Stevie, making certain to keep her voice low so that George wouldn't overhear. "I mean, is Miss Fenton going to assign them, or . . ."

"Good question!" Stevie raised her hand before Callie could even finish, waving it back and forth over her head as Miss Fenton explained that while each couple would receive a rating at the end of the week, it wouldn't count toward any actual grades since the project was just an experiment that year.

"But you will be expected to take this as seriously as any other school assignment," the headmistress finished sternly. Then, finally noticing Stevie's wildly waving hand, she nodded her way. "Yes, Stephanie?"

"So how's this going to work?" Stevie asked. "Do we get to pick our own hubbies, or are you going to play matchmaker?"

Miss Fenton pursed her lips. "I was getting to that," she said. "We've already done the pairings randomly, with the help of the office computer. You'll be assigned your partners this afternoon at the first meeting."

Callie let out the breath she hadn't even realized she was holding. *Whew!* she thought, still not daring to glance George's way. *That's a relief.*

She was so happy that she laughed out loud when Alex started making dire predictions about what would happen if he ended up paired with his twin sister. Maybe this marriage project sounded a little lame, but at least she wouldn't be stuck with George as her partner—not unless the fates, and the school computer, were *really* against her.

Even better, if we're both busy with our respective spouses, maybe he won't have time to follow me around everywhere and pretend not to be staring at me, she thought. *And that would definitely be good news.*

Callie smiled at the thought. She had enough on her mind this week, her first week back in training, without having to worry about fending off her not-so-secret admirer yet again.

THREE

When Lisa arrived at Pine Hollow that day after school, she found Alex pulling on his riding boots in the student locker room, the large, square room just off the main entryway where regular riders were assigned cubbyholes to stow their schoolbags and other items while they were at the stable.

Alex glanced up as she entered. "Hi, gorgeous," he greeted her with his usual lopsided smile.

There were several younger riders in the room, but Lisa hardly noticed them. She was totally focused on her boyfriend. Ever since her return from California, she'd thought of little else but making things work with Alex. She'd chosen her outfit carefully that day, knowing that the snug black leggings she was wearing flattered her slender figure and that her brick red wool turtleneck was Alex's favorite. The form-fitting outfit, which was definitely sexier than her usual weekday wardrobe, had meant a few extra stares and whistles from some of the more Neanderthal types at school, but it was all worth it the moment she saw her boyfriend's gaze slide down her body with obvious appreciation.

"Hi," she returned his greeting, walking over and bending down for a kiss.

Alex started to stand at the same time Lisa leaned in closer, and they bumped noses as their lips met. A little startled, Lisa jumped back, rubbing her nose. *It doesn't mean anything,* she thought. *Just lack of practice. And that's definitely something we can fix.*

But somehow, she didn't quite feel like giving it another try just then. After all, her idea of a romantic kiss wasn't standing in the middle of a locker room with a whole gang of younger riders staring and giggling.

"Just about ready for our ride?" she asked, turning toward her cubbyhole quickly and pretending not to notice that Alex was reaching for her again. She rummaged through the cubby, searching for her all-weather riding gloves. It was hard to believe that it was already the first week in December, but the chill in the air as she'd walked from her car to the stable building had told her that she'd better start accepting that winter was coming.

"Sure." Alex gave his left boot one last yank and then stood, shooting her a worried glance. "You okay? You look a little bummed. Is it your mom?"

Lisa felt a rush of emotion at the concern in his hazel eyes. How many girls were lucky enough to have such a sensitive, understanding boyfriend? "Mom's out of control," she admitted. "She took a few days off from work—says she needs time to 'get back in touch with herself.' Whatever that means." Lisa grimaced. Her mother had picked up a lot of those squishy self-help terms in her postdivorce group therapy.

Alex shook his head. "Bad news," he said sympathetically. "I can see why you're worried. I mean, I'm no shopping expert or anything, but even I know that the time between Thanksgiving and Christmas is, like, major."

"Uh-huh." Lisa headed across the wide entryway toward the hallway that led to the tack room, stable offices, and rest rooms. "And believe me, the last thing Mom needs is to lose her job right now, on top of everything else."

"Look on the bright side," Alex said with a small smile. "The store's probably so busy these days that the last thing her boss will want to do is fire someone."

Lisa knew he was trying his best to make her feel better, but it wasn't working. "I guess," she said quickly as they reached the tack room. She took a deep breath of the familiar leather-and-saddle-soap smell, then stepped forward to take a bridle off a hook on the wall. "Come on, let's hurry and hit the trail, okay? I just want to forget all about Mom and have a nice ride."

Alex shrugged agreeably. "Sure," he said. "I'll meet you out front in a few minutes."

Lisa felt a little strange as she grabbed a saddle and hurried out of the room without waiting for her boyfriend. Why did things seem so weird and off-kilter between the two of them? And worse yet, why didn't Alex seem to notice?

Maybe because it's all in my head, Lisa thought as she walked back across the entryway and entered the wide stable aisle. *I'm just feeling out of it because Alex and I haven't had much chance to be together for the past month or two. First we kept having all those stupid fights, then Alex got grounded, and then I was away last week. And now there's this business with Mom distracting me, just when things should be back to normal again. . . .*

She sighed, hoping that was all that was wrong. Stopping in front of a stall halfway down the aisle, she waited for the silvery gray mare inside to come to the front of the stall. "Hey there, Eve," she greeted the horse softly, rubbing her velvety nose. "Ready for some exercise?"

A few minutes later she and Alex were leading their horses toward the mounting block in the stable yard. That day Alex had tacked up one of his favorite mounts, a steady Appaloosa named Chip. As Lisa paused to adjust Eve's reins, she heard the sound of a car pulling into the gravel driveway a few dozen yards away. Glancing up, she recognized Scott Forester's dark green sports car.

er, too. "Hey, looks like Scott's car
       mechanic," he commented. "Guess
       nd Callie won't have to bum any
       Stevie and me."
       e here to pick up Callie," Lisa com-
       wrinkled her nose. "They must have
       ignals crossed, though. I think Callie
       for the trails on Barq."
       shrugged. "She did. She said she'd be out for
a couple of hours, at least."

"Really?" Lisa was surprised. She knew that Callie
was eager to start conditioning herself and Barq, but
a two-hour trail ride seemed a little extreme for their
first day of training. Still, she reminded herself that
Callie was the endurance expert, not her. Lisa was
sure her friend knew what she was doing.

As Scott climbed out of his car, he looked their
way and waved. A moment later he had joined them,
slightly breathless. "Hi, you two."

"Hi yourself," Lisa said, and Alex nodded.

Scott leaned over and punched him gently on the
shoulder. "Hey," he said with a sly wink. "So did you
tell your girlfriend there about your new wife?"

"I was about to." Alex grinned and glanced at Lisa.
"Hope you won't be jealous, sweetie, but I got
hitched today. Her name's Iris."

Lisa glanced from one guy to the other, feeling
confused. "What are you talking about?"

Alex quickly filled her in on the ma[...] "I got matched with this girl named [...] barely know her."

"I used to know her," Lisa said. "We went [...] munity tennis camp together for a couple o[...] back in elementary school. She's, uh, nice. I gue[...]

Scott grinned. "Yeah, that's my impression, too[...] he said. "I don't think I've heard her say two words since I've known her."

Coming from anyone else in Scott's situation, Lisa thought, it would have been a strange comment. After all, Scott had lived in Willow Creek for only a few months. He probably didn't even have any classes with Iris, since he was a senior.

But Scott's probably gotten to know more people in Willow Creek in the last six months than I have in the last seventeen and a half years, Lisa told herself, hiding a smile by turning to pat Eve, who was shifting her weight and gazing at Scott nervously. *He definitely inherited his father's charisma. Maybe he'll follow in his footsteps and go into politics as a career someday.*

"So who did everyone else get paired with?" she asked. "What about Stevie?"

Alex and Scott burst out laughing. "Talk about an odd couple!" Alex exclaimed. "She's married to Spike Anderson."

Lisa raised one eyebrow. "Spike?"

"His real name is Miles," Alex explained. "But everyone calls him Spike because he's this, like, amazing beach volleyball player. He's also a forward on our soccer team. You know, big guy, white-blond hair . . ."

"Oh, right." Lisa attended Alex's games whenever she could, and she quickly realized who he was talking about. "Wait a minute. Isn't he the one who celebrated your win at Homecoming by ripping off his uniform and taking a lap of the field in his underwear?"

"One and the same," Alex confirmed.

Lisa grinned. "Should be an interesting marriage."

Scott laughed again and took a step closer to pat Lisa on the arm. "Let's just say Stevie may be needing all the support she can get from her friends for the next week," he joked.

"So what about Callie?" Alex asked, swaying slightly as Chip nosed him in the shoulder before returning his attention to the snippet of grass between the mounting block and the schooling ring fence. "Who'd she get? I didn't hear."

"My sister was much luckier than yours," Scott replied. "She got paired up with Corey Westbrook. Do you know him?" He glanced at Lisa.

She nodded. Corey was a nice, smart guy who dated a classmate of Lisa's named Amelia LaRue. "He's a good guy. I know his girlfriend—she's in my computer class."

"Hmmm," Alex said. "I wonder if having a girlfriend counts against you as a husband?" He reached

41

over and squeezed Lisa's shoulder. "If so, Corey and I may both be in trouble."

Lisa smiled. "So what are you doing here, anyway?" she asked Scott, turning to tighten Eve's girth. "Alex says Callie's out on the trail."

"That's right," Alex confirmed. "Lorraine Olsen gave both of us a ride over here right after school. Callie seemed really eager to get started with her training."

"That's Callie for you." Scott shrugged and dug into his pocket. "I just stopped by to drop off her extra riding gloves—she left them in my car before I took it in to the mechanic. She probably totally forgot where she put them." He laughed fondly, shaking his head. "She's so psyched about getting back into training that she'll probably forget to come home for dinner if I don't come back and drag her away in a couple of hours."

Lisa glanced at him over her shoulder. "I'm sure if you leave her gloves in the office, Max or someone will make sure she gets them. Or you could just stick them in her cubby."

Scott nodded agreeably. "Guess I'll head inside then," he said. "Have a nice ride."

"Thanks." As Scott waved and wandered toward the stable entrance, Lisa returned most of her attention to Eve, though she also continued to think about the Fenton Hall marriage project.

It sounds like an interesting experiment, she

thought, holding Eve back so that Alex could lead his horse forward to mount. *Especially considering all the thinking I've been doing lately about marriage and families.*

Even now that she was home again, Lisa couldn't seem to stop mulling over everything that had happened during her trip to California. Her brother's new marriage had been a huge surprise to everyone. Besides that, Lisa had found it difficult to warm up to her new sister-in-law, Greta, and Greta's children. All the sudden changes made her think about the other ways her family had changed in the last few years, including her parents' divorce and her father's remarriage.

Why is it that things always seem to change just when you think you've got everything under control? Lisa wondered, thinking of her mother's breakup. *It's like you can't even relax for a minute without life kicking you upside the head. . . .*

"Lisa? Earth to Lisa!"

Lisa snapped out of her funk to find Alex in the saddle, staring at her. "Oops!" she said sheepishly. "Sorry. Guess I drifted off there for a sec." She quickly led Eve forward and mounted, keeping her face averted. She didn't feel like sharing her thoughts with Alex just then. She just wanted to hit the trail, have a nice time with her boyfriend, and forget about everything else for a while.

As they set off, heading for one of their favorite

trails in the woods beyond the big south pasture, Lisa couldn't help noticing how much more confident her boyfriend was in the saddle these days. He'd only started riding the previous spring, after they'd gotten together, because he wanted a way to spend more time with her. But lately he actually seemed to be enjoying it for its own sake, too. Lisa was happy about that. She didn't like the thought of asking him to do something he hated just so they could be together.

Still, that sort of thing would probably get him extra points if our relationship were part of the marriage project, she thought with a secret smile. *Actually, after all the stuff we've been through together lately, we'd probably end up at the top of the class.*

Her thoughts drifted from imaginary wedding bells to the real thing. She'd daydreamed plenty of times about what it would be like to be married to Alex. Sometimes she pictured the house they might buy together, or romantic dinners in front of the fireplace, or shopping for baby clothes. But today, for some reason, she couldn't bring up those images with any clarity. The only thing she could think about was the two of them leaning toward each other to kiss . . . and missing.

Stevie rushed into Pine Hollow Stables, her car keys still in her hand. The place was quiet for a weekday afternoon, and her footsteps echoed loudly on the wooden floorboards of the entryway. After a quick glance into the locker room, which was empty, she raced toward the tack room.

As she careened around the corner, the first person she spotted was Ben Marlow. The young stable hand was sweeping the floor outside the stable office. "Ben!" Stevie cried excitedly. "Where is everyone?"

Ben tossed back a thick shock of dark hair and glanced up at her, his face as impassive as ever "*Every-one?*" he repeated.

Stevie wasn't sure, but she thought she detected the faintest hint of a twinkle in his deadpan expression. *Could it be?* she wondered in amazement. *Could grumpy old Ben actually have a sense of humor in there somewhere?*

She didn't have time to worry about that at the moment, though. She was bursting to share her news with someone. "Okay, forget about everyone," she said briskly, jigging from one foot to the other. "I'll settle for Lisa, or Alex, or Callie. Have you seen them?"

Ben shrugged, returning his attention to his broom. "Lisa and Alex are out on the trails," he said in his usual brusque way. "Callie too. She won't be back for a while. Training." He shrugged again, and Stevie thought she saw his frown deepen. "That brother of hers. He's here—*again*. Back paddock."

Okay, so I guess that means Ben's stand-up routine is over, Stevie thought, resisting the urge to roll her eyes

45

at Ben's undisguised animosity toward Scott. She would never understand Ben Marlow. He seemed determined to be hostile and gloomy most of the time. Aside from horses, nothing seemed to give him any real pleasure, as far as Stevie could tell. That certainly wasn't the way she would want to go through life.

"Thanks," she told Ben shortly. "See you."

She hurried through the stable, stopping at Belle's stall just long enough to give her horse a quick pat and a promise of more attention later. As soon as she exited through the back door, she spotted Scott leaning against the post-and-board fence of the small back paddock. He was watching a couple of Pine Hollow's ponies as they dozed in the middle of the ring, enjoying the meager December sunshine.

"Hey!" Scott turned to greet Stevie with his usual easy, charming grin. "Where's the fire?"

Stevie skidded to a stop in front of him. "I don't know," she replied breathlessly. "But someone else will have to cover it. Because I've already got an assignment!"

Scott looked a little confused for a moment. Then his expression cleared. "Oh!" he said. "You mean for the *Sentinel*?"

"Yep," Stevie replied proudly. She flopped against the fence beside him, leaning over to catch her breath. "I had another meeting with Theresa just now, and I talked her into letting me write about the junior marriage project."

"Cool!" Scott looked impressed. "But I thought she wasn't going to let you write until, like, the next decade."

Stevie grinned. She'd spent most of chemistry class that day muttering to Scott, her lab partner, about how unfair Theresa was being. "I changed her mind," she explained. "I can be very persuasive, you know." She was only half kidding about that. She was genuinely proud of her ability to talk almost anyone into almost anything. Then she relented. "Actually, she didn't exactly promise she'd run my piece. But she said since all the other reporters are already working on stories for this issue, and this marriage project just came out of nowhere, I could take a shot at it, and she'd see."

"Good for you," Scott said sincerely. "I'm sure you'll be able to come up with something that will really wow her, Stevie." A sly grin crept across his face. "That is, if you can tear your attention away from your darling hubby long enough to write it."

Stevie grimaced. She'd been doing her best to forget about her marriage partner. "Very funny," she said. "If there's a *less* compatible husband for me in the entire state of Virginia than Spike Anderson, I can't imagine who it would be."

"Oh, I don't know." Scott smirked. "Don't they say

opposites attract? And a lot of girls seem to think Spike's some kind of hunk. . . ."

"Yeah," Stevie said sourly. "A hunk of dead brain cells."

Scott laughed. "Glad to see you're beginning your marriage all optimistic and dewy-eyed, Lake."

"Thanks, Forester. Now, can we get back to talking about my big break?" Stevie chewed on her lip, her gaze straying to the drowsy ponies, who were ambling slowly toward them. "I mean, I'm sure you're right and I can come up with a killer article by the Thursday deadline. I want to make it so thrilling that Theresa won't be able to resist printing it." She shrugged. "I'm just not sure I've hit on the right angle yet." Suddenly she brightened, realizing that she'd lucked onto the perfect brainstorming partner. Scott's whole family had plenty of experience with the media, thanks to Congressman Forester's high-profile job. If anyone could help her figure out the best way to approach her article, it was Scott. "So how about it?" she asked, glancing over at him. "Any brilliant ideas?"

Scott nodded thoughtfully, leaning back on his elbows against the paddock fence. "If you want to get people's attention on a sort of broad issue, it's usually best to zoom in on the personal level."

"What do you mean?" Stevie shot him a puzzled look as a pony named Penny reached the fence and stretched her neck over to give Stevie a curious sniff.

"You mean, like ask people what they think of the project as part of the article?"

"Well, maybe," Scott said. "But I was thinking more of an overall approach. A way to make people feel more involved in what the project is about by focusing on how it affects specific individuals."

Stevie stood up straight, shoving Penny's nose out of her left jacket pocket, where the pony was searching for treats. "I get it!" she exclaimed. "Like how in a lot of news stories in magazines and stuff, they'll start out by saying, like, 'So-and-So Smith is the fourth generation of his family to work as a farmer,' and then talk about that for a while before they get to the boring stuff about farm subsidies or whatever."

"Exactly." Scott smiled. "Trust me, I've been the subject of a few of those stories myself. They get people's attention."

Stevie nodded thoughtfully. "I could pick, say, three couples and follow their progress all week," she said. "Then I could sort of profile them, with all the intimate details of their 'marriages,' as a way of explaining what the project was all about and how it worked out."

"Perfect. So who are you going to profile?"

Stevie sighed. "Well, I hate to say it, but I guess one of the couples should be me and Spike." She made a sour face. "Not that I'm looking forward to that. But at least it will help show how even the most mismatched couple can work together and get through the project, right?"

"Sure," Scott said with a shrug. "Who else?"

"How about Callie?" Stevie suggested, reaching into her right jacket pocket just in time to rescue the small notebook she'd tucked there from Penny, who was exploring again. Flipping the notebook open and unclipping the pen she'd attached to it, she jotted down Callie's name. "She'll be a good subject, since she'll be willing to talk to me as much as I want. Besides, she and Corey are both so smart and responsible, they'll make a great contrast to me and Spike."

Scott laughed. "True," he agreed. "And I think Callie would definitely go along with it. She's not big on publicity most of the time, but I know she'll want to help you out on this."

Stevie nodded, sticking her pen in her mouth and chewing on the end as she pondered who her third couple should be. As her gaze strayed over the back paddock into the larger field off to one side, she spotted a sleek Trakehner mare grazing in the group that was turned out there. George Wheeler's horse, Joyride.

"How about George?" she said. "He got matched with Sue Berry, remember? I'm sure both of them would cooperate."

To her surprise, Scott shrugged. "I don't know," he said doubtfully. "I mean, yeah, George would be an easy subject. So would your brother and Iris. But that may not be the way to go if you want Theresa to take you seriously."

Stevie understood immediately. "Right," she said. "If I interview all my friends, I guess the article won't exactly be balanced, will it? Not that I count Spike Anderson as a close personal buddy or anything, husband or not." She rolled her eyes, then sighed and stared at her notebook. "But who else could I do who would be interesting and different?"

Instead of answering, Scott glanced over Stevie's shoulder toward the stable building. "Hey, Nicole," he called with a smile. "How's it going?"

Glancing back, Stevie saw Nicole Adams emerging from the back entrance, leading a bay gelding named Diablo. "Hi, you two!" Nicole trilled, waving at Stevie and Scott. "What's up?"

Stevie let out a grunt that she hoped would pass for a greeting. She and Nicole had known each other for most of their lives, but they had never really hit it off. Besides, Stevie's recent suspicions that Nicole might have a more-than-friendly interest in her brother didn't make her feel any warmer toward her vivacious, flirtatious classmate.

"Looks like you're ready to hit the trails," Scott commented to Nicole in his usual easy manner. "Where are you—"

"Hey!" Stevie interrupted suddenly as an idea struck her. "Nicole, who's your partner for the marriage project?" She shot Scott an eager glance. The answer to her problem could be standing right in front of her! After all, Nicole ran with Veronica's snobby, popular crowd—nobody could accuse Stevie's article of being too narrow in focus if it included her as one of its subjects. Plus, Nicole had just started taking lessons at Pine Hollow, so Stevie would have no trouble tracking her down for interviews.

Nicole giggled and blushed. "I got lucky," she confided. "My husband is Wesley Ward."

Stevie grimaced, her brilliant solution sliding down the drain immediately. Wesley was one of Spike's best friends. *No way do I want to deal with two stupid, immature jocks this week*, she thought. *One's going to be bad enough.*

Nicole was gazing at her suspiciously through her fringe of mascara-laden lashes. "Why do you ask?"

"Oh, no reason." Stevie smiled weakly. "Just curious."

Nicole shrugged, then glanced over at Diablo, who was pricking his small, batlike ears at the ponies. "Okay, I'd better get going," she said. "It gets dark early these days, and I really want to do some work on my lead changes."

"See you," Scott said, reaching forward to give Diablo a pat. "Have fun."

As Nicole moved on, one of the ponies, a slightly swaybacked gray named Nickel, came forward and nudged Scott's shoulder. Scott turned to pat the little gelding, then shot Stevie a glance. "So let me guess," he began. "When you heard who Nicole's partner was, you decided you didn't want to—"

Suddenly Stevie had a very interesting, slightly wicked idea. "I've got it!" she broke in, so abruptly that Nickel pulled his head back in surprise. "Veronica!"

Scott wrinkled his nose. "Veronica diAngelo? Are you saying you want to write about *her*?" he asked in surprise. "Forgive me if I'm wrong, but I thought you and Veronica didn't get along that well. Why would you want to voluntarily spend more time with her?"

Stevie grinned. "Because she got paired with Zach Lincoln," she explained. "You know, as in Blinkin' Lincoln, class spaz and the last guy on earth Veronica would ever talk to if she didn't have to."

Scott raised one eyebrow dubiously. "Well, at least no one could accuse you of only featuring your friends."

"I know. Besides, it will drive Veronica crazy to have her not-so-perfect match publicized, especially since she probably would've loved to get paired up with someone like Spike, or even Corey." Stevie scribbled a few lines in her notebook, her mind already churning with descriptive phrases for Veronica and her new husband.

Scott still looked a bit skeptical, but he didn't comment further on Stevie's third couple. "Well, it sounds like you're well on your way," he said, stroking Nickel's pale gray nose. "And by the way, congrats again on talking Theresa into giving you a shot."

"Thanks. And thanks for your ideas about the article, too." Stevie snapped her notebook shut and tucked it away before smiling at Scott gratefully. "I'm just glad I found you in time. If I hadn't found someone to tell about this when I did, I probably would've exploded. And then who would they give the Pulitzer Prize to this year?"

Scott grinned. "Glad I could be here for you, Stevie."

"Me too," Stevie said. Suddenly something occurred to her. "Hey, but what are you doing here, anyway? Ben said Callie's still out on the trail doing the endurance thing."

"Yeah, I know." Scott shrugged and pulled his jacket sleeve away from Nickel's curious teeth. "But I had to come by anyway to drop something off for her, so I figured, why make the trip twice? I thought I'd just hang out and offer my brilliant insights to any potential newspaper stars who happened by." He grinned and winked mischievously.

Stevie was a little surprised. Maybe she'd misunderstood, but from what Ben had told her, she doubted that Callie would be ready to leave any time soon. "Well, since I'm the only one of those you're likely to run into by the back paddock, why don't you go ahead and take off?" she offered. "I want to tell Lisa my news when she gets back, so I'll probably be here for a while yet, and I have the car today. I can run Callie home if you have other stuff to do."

"Thanks, but that's okay," Scott replied. "I don't mind hanging out here for a while." He grinned again. "Besides, if I'm here, Mom can't make me clean out my closet like she's been threatening all month."

Stevie shrugged and let it drop, though she was pretty sure he was just being diplomatic. She knew that Scott and Callie got along really well most of the time, but even so, it had to be tough on Scott to have to drive his sister around constantly. Stevie knew how that could be—it was difficult enough coordinating the use of the car she shared with Alex. The only thing that saved them from more fights than they already had over it was that their house was just a ten-minute walk from Pine Hollow. The Foresters lived in the same neighborhood, but for a long time even that short distance had been too much for Callie's weak leg, so Scott had been driving her over to the stable almost every day for the past few months.

"Now that Callie's leg is strong enough to let her drive again, it's too bad she doesn't have her own car so you wouldn't have to play chauffeur all the time," Stevie commented.

"I don't mind," Scott said. "Besides, she'll probably start shopping for a new endurance horse before long. Mom and Dad practically promised to buy her one when we moved here—that's why they leased Fez last summer, remember? And Callie will want the best. Whichever horse she settles on will probably cost as much as my car did, if not more."

Stevie nodded, feeling a momentary flash of envy. Her parents were both successful lawyers, and Stevie knew that she was more fortunate than most people—after all, she had her own horse, along with a nice home, a backyard swimming pool, and plenty of other luxuries. But with one child in college and two more just a year and a half from enrolling, the Lakes weren't exactly rushing out to buy expensive sports cars and competition-level Arabians, either.

"Good point," she told Scott, swallowing her envy. She knew that there was a trade-off to Callie and Scott's high-dollar lifestyle. Living in the public eye, knowing that they were always being watched because of who their father was, put pressures on them that Stevie and her other friends couldn't begin to imagine. "So do you really think she'll start looking for a new horse soon?"

Scott shrugged. "I don't see why not. She was pretty gung ho before the accident, and when Callie sets her mind to something . . ."

He didn't bother to finish, but Stevie nodded in agreement. Callie was one of the most intense people Stevie knew. *I mean, who else would kick off their return to training with an afternoon-long session out on the trails?* Stevie thought. *I'm sure Callie knows what she's doing and all, but it still seems pretty extreme.*

She shrugged that off, though. Callie could take care of herself. And right now Stevie had other things to think about—like trying to control her excitement about her article until Alex, Lisa, and Callie returned from their rides. She couldn't wait to tell them about it.

I'm just lucky Scott decided to hang around this afternoon, Stevie thought as she pulled her notebook out again, eager to get started. Maybe Scott could help her come up with interview questions for her subjects. *Because I wasn't kidding—if he hadn't been here to talk to, I really might have exploded!*

FOUR

As Carole turned onto her street, she spotted a familiar maroon sedan pulling into her driveway. *Looks like Dad's home early from his board meeting,* she thought, hitting her turn signal. Colonel Hanson had had a long and distinguished career in the Marine Corps before retiring a couple of years earlier. Since then he'd joined the boards of several charities and launched a second career making motivational speeches to businesses and other groups.

"Hi, honey," Colonel Hanson called as Carole climbed out of her car. "How was your volunteer meeting?"

"Good." Carole had recently started donating some of her free time to a local volunteer group called Hometown Hope. "We're going to start sprucing up the animal shelter on Saturday."

She'd only started volunteering with the group to avoid being suspended from school. But Carole had to admit that working with Hometown Hope was turning out to be a lot more rewarding than she ever would have expected. *Besides,* she thought, *all the scrubbing and painting I'm going to be doing this weekend will give me plenty of time to figure out my future.*

During her fourth-period study hall, Carole had tried to follow Lisa's advice by making out a list of all the horse-related careers she could imagine. By the time the list was two pages long, she'd started to feel a little overwhelmed. How was she ever going to decide? Just about the only conclusion she'd come to so far was that becoming an equine vet probably wasn't for her. That had always been high on her list, mostly because she really admired Judy Barker, the vet who cared for the horses at Pine Hollow. A few years earlier, Carole had even spent some time going on rounds with Judy, assisting in everything from foaling to euthanasia and learning more than she ever would have imagined.

But as much as Judy's knowledge and dedication inspired her, Carole didn't think she was cut out to follow in her footsteps. For one thing, being a vet really wouldn't play to her strengths—riding, training, and general horse care. She would have to focus so much on equine health that she might not have a lot of time left over to spend on those things. *And speaking of time, there's one other time problem with becoming a vet,* she thought as she hoisted her backpack onto her shoulder. It was stuffed with textbooks she needed for that night's homework. *That's the time I'd need to spend in school. It would take years and years of sitting in classrooms, taking tests, and writing papers. I'm not sure I'm cut out for all that extra schooling.*

"Do you have your house key handy?" Colonel Hanson said, breaking into her thoughts. "We got so much mail today, I need both hands just to hold it." He shook his head in dismay as he flipped through the thick stack of mail. "Is it just me, or do we get about seventeen times as many catalogs at this time of year?"

Carole smiled. "I don't think it's just you," she replied. "It's because there are only twenty-three shopping days until Christmas."

Her father glanced up from the stack of mail, looking startled. "Really?" he said. "How did you know that?"

Carole laughed at his expression. "I don't," she admitted. "It was just a guess."

Colonel Hanson grinned. "I should have known," he teased. "I mean, most people would be able to figure it out from today's date. But since when does my scatterbrained daughter remember what day it is—or what month, for that matter?"

Carole shrugged and smiled. It was true that she rarely remembered what day of the month it was unless she had a horse show to attend or something important going on at the stable. But these days she was finding it much easier to keep track of the passing days. Still, she didn't think it was necessary to mention that she knew exactly how many days were left until New Year's, which signaled the end of her grounding.

Besides, she didn't want to think about that at the moment. It would only ruin her mood. And her mood just then was actually pretty good for a change. The volunteer meeting had gone well, and she'd aced the biology quiz her teacher had handed back that day. Besides, as she stepped ahead, house key in hand, Carole couldn't help thinking that it felt really good to be on more comfortable terms with her father once again. After Colonel Hanson had found out about the cheating incident, Carole had really started to wonder whether things would ever go back to normal between them. They'd always been close, and in the years since Carole's mother had died of cancer, they had become as much friends as father and daughter.

I guess we're not quite back to that point yet, Carole thought as she turned the key in the lock and led the way into the house. But the week before at Thanksgiving dinner, they'd finally cleared the air between them. Talking out their recent problems had made the atmosphere at home a lot more pleasant.

"You're home early, Dad," she commented, dropping her backpack on the floor and shrugging off her coat. "How was your board meeting?"

"It was fine," Colonel Hanson replied, still sorting through the mail as Carole headed to the hall closet to hang up her coat. "There really wasn't much new business to discuss this time, so we . . ."

His voice drifted off, and Carole glanced over her shoulder. Her father's expression was very strange. "What's the matter?"

Colonel Hanson held up a thin white envelope. "This is for you."

"What is it?" Carole was confused. She didn't get much mail aside from horse magazines and catalogs. Glancing at the return address as she accepted the envelope didn't help her much.

Her father cleared his throat. "Looks to me like it's your PSAT scores."

Carole gulped, staring at her name on the envelope. *I almost forgot about the PSATs,* she thought with a rush of nervousness. The entire junior class had taken the standardized test a few weeks earlier. Even though it was just a preliminary test to help prepare them for taking the SATs that spring, Carole knew that her score on the PSATs was still pretty important. For one thing, it was the first step in getting ready to apply to colleges the following year. *But more to the point right now,* she added as she turned the envelope over in her hands, still staring at its blank whiteness, *it could blow things between me and Dad again, just when we're getting back on track. He's so into the importance of a good education and all that stuff—if I bombed on this, he'll freak out. And then who knows when I'll see Pine Hollow again.*

Glancing up, she saw that her father was staring at her eagerly, the rest of the mail forgotten. Knowing she couldn't put it off any longer, Carole took a deep breath and slid her finger under the flap of the envelope.

"Too bad Callie decided not to come," Lisa commented, scanning the menu a waitress had just handed her. She, Alex, Stevie, and Scott were crowded into a small booth at TD's, their favorite ice cream parlor. "Isn't mint chocolate chip her favorite flavor? It's the special today—two scoops for the price of one."

Stevie looked interested. "Really?" she said. "Mint chocolate chip's kind of boring, but I'm just starved enough to go for that right now."

Lisa's stomach grumbled. After her long trail ride through the crisp afternoon air, she was hungry, too. And knowing that her mother wasn't likely to be up to cooking dinner in her current state, she planned to fill up now. She almost wished that they'd decided to stop for a snack at a pizza place or sandwich shop rather than the ice cream parlor.

"You know," she commented, "some people might think eating ice cream when it's, like, forty degrees outside is kind of weird."

Alex cocked an eyebrow at her. "Are any of those people here right now?"

"No way." Scott laughed. "I know I'm definitely in

the mood for a triple banana split. And I don't care if it's twenty below zero outside."

Lisa chuckled. Scott could probably convince Eskimos to switch to an all-ice-cream diet if he put his mind to it. "Actually, a banana split sounds perfect," she said. "Maybe I'll have one, too."

"Me three," Alex put in, tossing his menu to the center of the table. He shrugged and grinned. "Now that I'm a married man, I'm going to have to get my junk food where I can. My new wife is some kind of health freak. She says we can only spend our family budget on organic vegetarian foods and purified water."

"Really?" Stevie laughed. "Did you tell Iris that your idea of the four food groups are sugar, salt, grease, and more grease?"

Alex rolled his eyes. "Get real, Stevie," he said. "The fourth group isn't more grease. It's caffeine, of course."

Lisa laughed. "Sounds like Iris might be a good influence on you," she teased. "I've been trying to get you to eat healthier for months. Maybe she'll have more luck."

"Guess again." Alex leaned over and planted a kiss on Lisa's temple. "Nobody has more influence over me than you, sweetie."

"Isn't that cute." Scott grinned at Stevie. "Looks like Alex's sudden marriage isn't hurting their relationship any, huh? I hope the same is true of you and Phil."

"Don't worry about us," Stevie replied as the waitress reappeared and set four glasses of water on the table. "It would take a lot more than getting married to someone else to mess us up. Especially now that Phil finally shook off that stupid pneumonia that kept him in bed for the entire break."

The waitress interrupted to ask for their orders, and once she left, the group continued to chat about the marriage project and other topics. But Lisa was only half listening.

I guess it's not surprising that I feel weird about Alex being "married" to another girl, even if it's just for a school project, she thought. *But it's not like I'm jealous or anything. I know that Alex would never be interested in someone like Iris.*

She shot her boyfriend a sidelong glance. He was leaning over the table, talking to Stevie and Scott, so he didn't notice her look. As usual, his brown hair was slightly rumpled and his eyes were bright, giving him the boyish, mischievous look that Lisa had always found irresistible.

So why do I keep thinking that the whole idea of arranged marriages suddenly doesn't sound so bad? she thought, toying with her napkin. *I mean, it's nuts. But with all the crazy and confused thoughts I've been having about me and Alex lately, it sure does seem like it would be a lot easier to have these kinds of decisions taken out of my hands.*

FIVE

Carole blinked, wondering if she was hallucinating.

Or maybe I wasn't paying enough attention when they told us what the scores mean, she thought. *Maybe it's like golf, where a low score is good and a high score is bad.* She wasn't completely positive that things worked that way in golf, but that just helped prove her point. After all, while she could have explained precisely how a dressage judge assigned points for any test from Training Level to Grand Prix, she wasn't too clear on the scoring of most non-equine sports, mostly because she didn't care all that much.

She glanced over at her father, who seemed to be having some sort of attack. His eyes were bulging and he was gasping for breath like a fish on a line.

"Carole!" he sputtered, his voice choked and raspy. "Do you realize what this means?"

Carole bit her lip, certain now that her golf theory was right. *I guess I can kiss Pine Hollow good-bye for a lot longer than another month,* she thought helplessly.

This academic stuff is so important to Dad. I guess I should have remembered that and studied a lot harder for this stupid test, no matter how busy I was with more interesting things—like everything, for instance. . . .

"Sorry, Dad," she began. "I really thought I did okay, but I guess—"

"Okay?" Colonel Hanson raised one hand to his forehead as if checking to make sure it was still there. "Okay? Carole, this score—it's *fantastic!*"

"It is?" Carole wrinkled her brow, puzzled. She glanced at the paper in her hand again. "You mean I didn't mess it up?"

Colonel Hanson reached out and grabbed her, pulling her in for a tight hug. "Oh, honey," he said, still sounding a little choked up. "If you do as well on the SATs as you did on this, you'll be able to get into any college you want. You could go to Harvard. Or Annapolis!"

Carole's head was spinning, and not just because her father's fierce hug was cutting off her breath. Harvard? Annapolis? It didn't compute. When she'd bothered to think about the PSATs at all, the most Carole had hoped for was an adequate score—one that would keep her father happy and set her up for a reputable equine studies program at a solid local university like NVU. She'd never imagined anything more.

Still, this is definitely good news, she thought as her father continued to babble about all her unlimited possibilities for the future. *I mean, anything that makes Dad this happy has got to be good news, right?*

"There you go, bub." Callie gave the lively Arabian gelding a pat on the neck. "Fresh as a daisy."

Barq didn't bother to respond. Instead he turned away from her as soon as she released him, nosing at his water bucket. Callie sighed, suddenly missing a particular horse she'd ridden regularly at her old stable back on the West Coast. The horse had been an Arab cross named Karachi, and he'd been one of the best horses she'd ever seen. He'd had an instinctive feel for the best path over a difficult trail, solid hooves that had never known a crack or split, and a will to win that was almost as strong as Callie's own.

"You're a good horse, fella," she murmured, scratching Barq at the base of his mane. "I'm just not sure you're going to do the trick for me. Not for long, anyway."

She sighed again. After that day's long workout, she was feeling less optimistic about getting back into competitive form with Barq. He was an Arabian, generally the most successful breed in endurance riding. The same efficient cooling system—thin skin and large blood vessels—that helped them survive in the harsh desert conditions under which the breed was developed, as well as their relatively light bones and natural stamina, made Arabians a popular choice for the strenuous sport of endurance riding. But a lot still depended on the individual. Most reasonably fit horses, Arabian or otherwise, could safely train for endurance races—maybe even win a local twenty-five-miler or two. But it took a special horse to compete at a higher level and win. A horse like Karachi. Or like Fez, the horse that had died on that rainy summer night when Callie's whole life had changed.

But the change was temporary, Callie thought fiercely, banishing the memories of that horrible moment when she'd felt the car spinning out of control on the slick road. *Now I'm back. Or I will be before long, anyway. Just as soon as I can find the horse to help me.*

After a quick check to make sure that Barq's water bucket was full enough, Callie let herself out of the stall and wandered slowly down the stable aisle, feeling weary and dissatisfied. Right next door to Barq was Starlight, Carole's bay gelding. *Nice horse,* Callie thought, stepping up to the stall and scanning Starlight's conformation as he dozed in the corner. *Good paces, and he certainly has good form over fences. But you can tell by his feet that he's part Thoroughbred. Those hooves belong in a show ring or on a smooth trail or pasture. Not on a tough, rocky ride over rough terrain where every second counts.*

Next in line was Belle, Stevie's horse. The feisty mare was hanging her head over the half door of her stall, watching Callie with bright, curious eyes. Callie stopped to give her a pat.

"Half Arabian," she murmured, leaning against the stall door and running her eyes down the mare's sleek, coppery neck. "So you've probably got some natural stamina, eh, girl? Not bad conformation. But that Saddlebred half . . ." She shook her head, taking in Belle's long pasterns. While Callie had seen gaited horses finish well in a few races, she knew that they weren't generally among the best of the best.

After giving the spirited mare one last pat, she moved on, realizing that it didn't really matter whether Belle or Starlight had endurance potential. They belonged to her friends, which meant they wouldn't be available for hours and hours of hard training and conditioning, potential or not.

Max's horses were another story. Callie was sure that the stable owner would let her work with just about any of his school horses. But were any of them good enough? Barq had seemed like the obvious choice, but now Callie wasn't so sure that any amount of work she could do with him would bring him or her to the necessary level.

She checked out a few other possibilities as she continued down the aisle. Comanche had spirit, but he had a choppy trot that would be difficult to ride for the extended periods required in endurance; and besides, he was getting on in years. Callie wasn't sure, but she guessed that the chestnut gelding was probably in his late teens. That was far from decrepit, but it was old enough when the horse had never been asked to finish a fifty-mile course over steep, rocky ground. Callie planned to train hard to get herself back in shape for competition, and she needed a horse that could keep up.

Congo was younger, but much too heavy to make him an efficient mover. Besides, he lacked the fire that Callie had always found so important in her competition mounts. While it didn't pay to have a hyper horse that would wear itself out before the ten-mile mark, it was definitely an advantage to have a horse with a winning spirit. All the training in the world couldn't give a horse that spark, and Congo just didn't have it.

Then there was Topside. The Thoroughbred gelding had been a show-jumping champion in his younger days, and he had impeccable manners. Callie had no doubt that she would be able to control him even in the most crowded shotgun start, or that he would accept her orders about pacing no matter how much he wanted to catch up to a speedier opponent. But like Comanche, he was a little past his prime for competition. Besides, as a Thoroughbred—and a large one at that—he was unlikely to be a contender among the tough little Arabians, Arab crosses, and mustangs that dominated the sport.

Windsor wasn't even a faint possibility. The big, handsome, dignified gelding was a perfect school horse for intermediate riders. He was kind and willing, but definitely not a pushover. However, his sheer size made him the wrong choice for Callie. Not only was he too big to make a likely endurance prospect, but he was too big for her to fit comfortably over a long, strenuous day of riding, though she had no trouble riding him for shorter periods.

Callie sighed as she glanced down the stable aisle, picturing herself trying to finish a fifty-mile ride on any of the rest of the horses housed on either side of the wide aisle, or the others that occupied the other arm of the U-shaped stable. Diablo. Checkers. Talisman. Calypso. Eve. Chip.

It's no use, she thought, grinding her teeth in frustration. *None of them is right for what I need to do. At least not from what I've seen of them.*

She couldn't just go home with the problem unresolved. Spinning on her heel, she headed toward the top of the aisle. She would go talk to Max. Maybe he would come up with a possibility she'd missed.

Halfway down the hall leading to the office, Callie heard Max's voice. It sounded as though he was talking on the phone.

". . . will have to hit the ground running, so I'll need someone who has quite a bit of experience," Max was saying.

The office door was open, so Callie stuck her head in and knocked softly on the frame. Glancing up from his seat behind his messy desk, Max gestured for her to enter.

"Yes, yes, that's excellent," he continued into the phone as Callie tiptoed in and took a seat in the guest chair. "How many years were you there?"

Sounds like he's talking to someone about the stable hand job, Callie thought, flicking a spot of mud off her jeans leg. *I almost forgot he's been trying to hire someone.* She knew that Max's search for a new Pine Hollow staffer was only partly because Carole had had to quit her job while she was grounded. The population of the Willow Creek area was growing, and the stable had been getting noticeably busier, even in the six months that Callie had been riding there. Max was talking about buying a few more horses to keep up with the demand, and Callie had even heard him mention possibly building an addition to the stable if things kept on the way they were going.

She tuned back in to Max's conversation. It sounded as though he was wrapping things up. "Okay, then," he said briskly. "Can you come by sometime this week so we can talk a little more in person? Say, Thursday at noon?" He nodded with a satisfied smile as he listened to the person on the other end of the line. "Great," he said. "See you then. Oh, and please wear riding clothes."

Max said good-bye and hung up. Then he glanced at Callie.

"Now," he said. "What can I do for you?" He checked his watch. "I thought all your cronies left a while ago. Something about ice cream?"

Callie waved one hand impatiently. She'd had absolutely no interest in sitting around stuffing herself with sugar along with her brother and the others. And she certainly didn't need Scott driving her home every time she came to the stable anymore, either. She'd insisted that the four of them go ahead without her, and to her relief, they'd agreed. "Uh-huh. Listen, Max. I'm kind of worried."

Max leaned back in his chair and crossed his hands behind his head. "What about?"

"Barq," Callie replied succinctly. She paused, thinking back once again over that day's ride. "I took him out for a long time today—you know, to see how we get along and what kind of condition he's in."

Max nodded. "Yes, I know," he said. "So I take it things didn't go well?"

"Not really." Callie shrugged. "Don't get me wrong, Barq's a nice horse. But I'm not sure he's going to be up to the task. His balance is okay, and I'm sure I could get him into shape on that, but he just doesn't seem to get what I want from him."

"It is your first day working together," Max reminded her gently.

Callie frowned. How could she explain it to him? "I know," she said. "Believe me, I know what you're saying. But what I'm saying is that I just don't get a good feeling about my chances with Barq. Like I said, he's a very nice horse. We just don't, I don't know, *click*."

Max nodded somberly. "I see." He leaned forward again, resting his elbows on the desk and running one hand over his short-cropped hair. "Well, that's a problem, then—at least if you're planning to take Barq all the way to competition level. But it will be a while before you need to worry about that. In the meantime, while you're getting yourself back into shape, I really think Barq is the best horse I have for your needs."

Callie frowned. That wasn't the answer she'd been hoping for. "Are you sure?" she asked. "I mean, isn't there another horse I should try before I make up my mind?"

"Well, let me see. If Chippewa were a few years younger, I'd suggest him," Max said, rubbing his chin and staring thoughtfully at the wall. "Appaloosas can be successful long-distance horses. Chip's legs and feet are rock solid, and his night vision has always been just fine. But I think he's getting a little long in the tooth to start a new discipline now."

Callie nodded. She'd already come to that conclusion herself, but she had to respect Max's knowledge of his own horses—and of the different requirements for seemingly every equine sport out there. Hearing about the wide range of disciplines and activities he'd had his young riders try over the years, from endurance riding to foxhunting to polocrosse, Callie had almost wished that she'd learned to ride at Pine Hollow, too.

"I know," she muttered. "And you're right. There's really no horse at Pine Hollow that's going to do better than Barq." She sighed. "I guess I'll just have to make do."

She thanked Max for his time and left the office, still feeling a bit disgruntled. *That's it, then,* she thought. *The only answer is to get myself a new horse—my own horse, a competition horse—as soon as possible. I'll have to start talking to Mom and Dad about it—*

"Hi, Callie!" A loud voice interrupted her thoughts.

Glancing up, Callie saw George Wheeler hurrying down the hallway toward her, a big grin on his round face. "Oh," she said, not in any mood to deal with George's crush on her. "Hi, George."

"I thought I heard you in there with Max." George beamed as he came to a stop beside her. "I figured I'd wait and say hi."

"Uh-huh." Callie continued on her way down the hall, with George matching her step for step. "Well, listen, I've got to get going. See you at school."

"I'll walk you out," George responded quickly. "Actually, I was getting ready to head home myself."

Callie bit back a sigh, thanking her lucky stars that George lived in the opposite direction from her—and that he didn't have a car. "Whatever," she muttered.

"So how's your training going?" George asked brightly, not seeming to notice her irritation.

Callie shrugged. "I've only been at it one day," she said a bit sharply.

George laughed and touched her lightly on the arm. "I know, I know," he said. "Sorry. But I just think endurance riding is interesting. I really want to learn all about it. In fact, if you need any help—you know, a riding partner or whatever—just let me know, because I—"

"Ben!" Callie blurted out, suddenly spotting her salvation stalking across the stable entryway in the form of Ben Marlow. She shot George what she hoped would pass for an apologetic smile. "Look, I really need to go talk to Ben for a sec. Um, about Barq."

"Oh." George's smile faded quickly. He shot Ben a cautious look. "Okay. Then I'll see you tomorrow, I guess." He slunk away quickly, disappearing through the stable entrance a second later.

Callie heaved a sigh of relief. She knew that George was intimidated by most other guys—especially strong, silent, brooding types like Ben. *Thank goodness that little trick worked,* she thought. Suddenly noticing that Ben had paused and was looking at her expectantly, Callie smiled sheepishly.

"Um, never mind," she told him quickly. "It's nothing. Really."

Ben didn't reply. He just shrugged and moved on, not even seeming curious about Callie's odd behavior.

Callie waited just long enough to ensure that she wouldn't run into George outside. Then she headed for the door herself, already forming her arguments for why her parents needed to let her start shopping for a horse as soon as possible.

SIX

"Yo, wife!" Spike greeted Stevie loudly, looking up as she approached his cafeteria table, where he was surrounded by his usual crowd of friends and admirers. "What's up, babe?"

Stevie sighed. *What did I ever do to deserve this?* she wondered. *My luck must really be on a downswing to get stuck with Spike Anderson for this project.*

She knew that a lot of girls at Fenton Hall would be quick to disagree. Even Stevie had to admit that Spike wasn't too hard on the eyes. He was a couple of inches over six feet tall, with a quick and winning, if slightly cocky, grin and light blond hair bleached even lighter by time spent in the sun. Along with his broad shoulders and the rangy muscles of a natural athlete, his other attributes included—according to a conversation Stevie had once overheard between Nicole Adams and one of her bimbo friends—the world's finest butt.

"So you couldn't stay away from hubby, eh?" Spike commented, much to the delight of his buddies.

"Well, if you want to make out, you'll have to wait till I finish my lunch." He held up his half-eaten sandwich.

Finest butt, yeah right, Stevie thought irritably. *If you ask me, the only award Spike deserves is world's biggest butt*-head!

"Very funny," she told him with a frown. "In case you forgot, we agreed to meet now to go over our assignment. Marriage class is next period, remember?"

"Oh, right." Spike smiled and winked at his friends. "That's what they all say." But he got up, gathering his lunch and following Stevie to an unoccupied table nearby.

As she took a seat across from him, Stevie swallowed a frustrated sigh. Taking care of the extra work for marriage class and coming up with brilliant ideas for her newspaper article at the same time wasn't turning out to be as easy as she'd hoped. The day before, Miss Fenton and the guest speaker, a professional marriage counselor, had asked the couples to meet and draw up their own wedding vows, expressing what they expected from the relationship.

That had sounded easy enough at first. But it turned out that Spike had a team meeting for the upcoming basketball season after school. Besides, Stevie had needed to meet with Theresa about her idea for the article. Spike wasn't sure how long his meeting would run, and Stevie hadn't wanted to waste time waiting around for him to finish when she could be at Pine Hollow. She'd offered to come by Spike's house after dinner, but he had a date. Finally they'd given up trying to work out a time and agreed to each write down some ideas on their own, which they had planned to combine somehow at lunch.

At least that's what I thought we'd agreed to, Stevie thought sourly as she flipped open her notebook. *Apparently, Spike forgot all about the assignment. It figures.* She was glad she'd managed to jot down a few notes while she was working on an outline for her *Sentinel* article. The last thing she wanted was to be caught totally unprepared in front of the entire junior class that afternoon.

"Okay," she said, trying to stay positive. She was going to make this ridiculous marriage work if it was the last thing she did. Otherwise it would be just too humiliating to include herself in her article, and changing her plan now would mess up the whole outline. "Listen up. Here's what I've got so far." She glanced at Spike to make sure he was paying more attention to her than to his sandwich. "I, Miles Anderson, do hereby solemnly swear to love and honor and adore Stevie Lake, and I promise on my life that this will be a partnership, with all the good stuff and the not-so-great stuff shared equally, like cooking and vacuuming and mowing the lawn or whatever."

Spike snorted. "That's the best you could come up

with? Totally pathetic!" he exclaimed. "Nope, here's what we're going to say." He cleared his throat dramatically and unfolded a slightly crumpled sheet of notebook paper. "I, Spike Anderson, Esquire, promise to honor and love Stevie Lake, to support her in style with my million-dollar endorsement deals, and to protect her from the dirty minds of other dudes when they hit on her. In return, I, Stevie Lake, swear to honor, worship, and obey my studly husband, the pinnacle of manliness, Spike Anderson, Esquire. I promise to cook for him, clean his house, do his laundry, wash his hair, and repair his nets when necessary. Oh, and also to always be available for, uh, the performance of my wifely duties." He smirked and wriggled his eyebrows suggestively.

"Give me that." Suddenly suspicious, Stevie snatched the sheet out of his hand. It was blank, except for the name *Melanie* and a phone number. "You didn't do the assignment at all, did you?"

Spike shrugged and raked one hand through his hair. "What's the big deal?" he said casually. "It's not like we get graded on this. Besides, I had a date last night, remember?"

"Yeah, I remember," Stevie snapped. "But you're sadly mistaken if you think I'm going to let your love life mess up this stupid marriage." As Spike grinned again, Stevie tossed her head and stood up. "You know what I mean. Anyway, just keep quiet in class today, okay? I'll come up with something for our vows so we don't end up looking like total idiots. In the meantime, I have better things to do than sit around here with you." Spotting Callie sitting alone at a table across the cafeteria, Stevie grabbed her notebook and stomped away without a backward glance.

I really hope Mom and Dad come around soon, Callie thought, taking a bite of her apple and flipping through the pages of the new book on endurance riding she'd received through the mail. It had arrived the day before, but she'd been so tired from her long day of training—not to mention her long evening of trying to convince her parents to let her start horse shopping—that she'd only made it through the first chapter before falling asleep. *Because the thought of starting Barq on a serious LSD program when he probably isn't cut out for endurance racing at all makes me want to cry.* LSD stood for long slow distance training, the conditioning that endurance riders did to get their horses into shape for the rigors of their sport. Callie knew that an LSD program would improve Barq's physical abilities on the trail, but it couldn't give him the will to win or the desire to keep pace for hours at a time for the sheer joy of it. No training program could do that.

Callie paused over a photo in the book. It showed a compact, tough-looking little mustang clambering its way up a steep rocky trail, its rider leaning so far forward in the saddle that she was almost eating mane.

Somehow, I can't see Barq taking that kind of tough incline in stride, Callie thought dejectedly, wishing that girl in the photo could be her. *Or any of the other horses at Pine Hollow, either. No matter how much training and conditioning I do.*

There was no question about it. She needed her own horse, a real endurance horse. Otherwise there was no way she would be competitive again anytime soon. Why couldn't her parents see that as clearly as she did? All they'd said the night before—despite all her convincing arguments, and even despite her respectable PSAT scores, which had arrived in the mail that afternoon—was "we'll think about it."

As Callie lowered the book to her lap and reached for her orange juice, she noticed Stevie barreling across the cafeteria toward her, a dark scowl on her face. "Hi," Callie said as Stevie reached her table. "Is something wrong?"

Stevie flopped into the empty seat across from Callie and snorted. "Yeah," she replied. "I'm married to an imbecile."

Callie gasped, suddenly remembering that she'd made plans for that lunch period—plans that had completely slipped her mind, thanks to all the other issues that were crowding it. "Oh no!" she cried, slamming her book closed and jumping to her feet. "I'm supposed to be meeting with Corey right now.

We need to finish up our vows. We did most of it on the phone last night, but we wanted to tighten up the wording today, and—Well, anyway, I'd better go find him."

"Oh! Wait. That reminds me." Stevie gave her a pleading smile. "Did Scott happen to mention anything to you yesterday about my new assignment for the *Sentinel*?"

Callie was busy scanning the cafeteria, trying to remember where Corey usually sat. Finally she spotted him sitting by himself at a table near the windows and waved. "Uh, what?" she asked Stevie as Corey waved back and smiled. Callie stuffed the rest of her apple into her paper lunch bag and tucked her book under her arm.

"My article," Stevie said insistently. "Did he tell you about it?"

Callie vaguely remembered Scott telling the family something about Stevie's big plans for some newspaper article at dinner the night before. Callie had been distracted by her own thoughts, so she hadn't really caught all of what he was saying. "Um, I think so," she said, glancing over at Corey again. He was still looking her way and smiling. She didn't want to keep him waiting any longer than she already had, especially since they only had about fifteen minutes left in the lunch period to finish their assignment. "He said, uh, you were writing about the marriage project. Right?"

"Right," Stevie confirmed. "I'm featuring three different couples, following their progress through the week and then seeing how things turn out for all of them. And I thought you and Corey would be perfect as one of the three couples. So what do you say?"

"Oh." Callie shrugged. "I guess that would be all right. I'll check with Corey and make sure he's okay with it if you want."

"Great!" Stevie looked pleased. "Thanks a lot, Callie. Maybe we can talk more about it this afternoon at Pine Hollow. I have a date with Phil tonight, but I was going to stop by for a quick ride first."

"Okay. See you later." Callie gave Stevie a little wave, grabbed her cane, which was leaning against the empty chair beside hers, and hurried over to Corey's table.

His brown eyes were twinkling as she approached. "Hey, Callie," he greeted her, a mischievous smile on his boyish face. "I was starting to think my new wife was already having an affair or something."

"I'm so sorry, Corey." Callie set her things down on the table and slid into a seat beside him. "I totally forgot we were supposed to meet today." She shrugged apologetically and gestured to her endurance book. "This came in the mail just yesterday, and I couldn't wait to read it, and, well . . . Anyway, I'm really sorry."

Corey picked up the book. "Endurance riding?" he said. "What's that?"

"It's my sport," Callie said. "I mean, I used to do it a lot before I moved here. You know, before the accident." She gestured in the general direction of her right leg, feeling a little self-conscious. "Anyway, endurance is basically long-distance trail riding. Most of the important races are fifty or one hundred miles long, and they're timed and everything."

"A hundred miles? Wow. Sounds like quite a sport." Corey looked impressed. Then he glanced at the large, old-fashioned clock on the wall above the cafeteria entrance. "Oops. But maybe you should tell me more about that later. We've only got a little while."

"I know. I'm sorry," Callie said again.

Corey grinned. "Don't sweat it," he said. "I'm in this marriage for better or for worse, remember?"

"Okay." Callie smiled back, glad that she'd ended up with such a nice, understanding partner.

Before long the two of them were poring over Corey's notebook, where he'd started sketching out their vows the night before. "Okay," Corey said. "I like the part where we both say we'll 'love, honor, and cherish.' Very traditional without being sexist."

"Uh-huh." Callie chewed on the end of her pen and read over what they had so far. "But we don't really say that much about what we expect from the marriage. That's part of the assignment, too."

"Good point." Corey buried one hand in his thick, straight brown hair and stared at the page thoughtfully. "I know if I were getting married for real, I'd probably want a real partner in life. Someone I could talk to about anything. Someone I could trust and respect and count on to be there for me, as well as someone to adore and worship and cherish and all that."

Callie nodded eagerly and started scribbling notes in the margins. "That sounds great. Very romantic, actually."

Before either of them could say anything else, there was a loud shriek from a nearby table. Startled by the sudden noise, Callie glanced over to see a popular cheerleader named Betsy Cavanaugh dancing around, clawing at her clingy cotton shirt and shrieking loudly. Spike Anderson and a few of his buddies were nearby, doubled over with laughter. When Wesley Ward darted forward and Callie spotted the ice cubes in his hand, she realized what had happened.

Corey was watching the scene, too. "Wow," he said wryly. "I guess some guys really know how to flirt, huh? Maybe I should try the old ice-cube-down-the-shirt trick out on Amelia sometime. I'm sure she'd be really impressed."

Callie chuckled and shook her head. "Yeah, right," she said. "I think that one stopped working on me when I graduated from kindergarten."

Poor Stevie, she thought as she and Corey returned their attention to their assignment. *I sure wouldn't want to be stuck with that dork Spike as a partner.* Just then a quick motion caught her eye. Glancing over, she saw George walking past their table. He was looking her way, a curious expression on his face. His steps slowed, and Callie was afraid he was going to come over and join them. *Of course, Spike wouldn't be my last choice for a fake husband. . . .*

She shuddered, flashing to the image of George hovering outside the stable office the previous day. What would she have done if they'd been paired for the marriage project? She didn't like to think about it. He was already practically her shadow.

"Hey," Corey said, waving a hand in front of her face. "Earth to Callie. Time to get back to talking about how incredibly romantic and handsome I am." He grinned.

Callie couldn't help laughing, even though she was still watching George out of the corner of her eye. He had come to a complete stop by now, just a few feet from their table. Any second now he would probably start heading toward her.

She forced herself to smile at Corey. "Yeah, right," she teased, trying to sound normal. "I don't remember saying anything about you being handsome."

Corey pretended to look hurt. "Oh, really? Well, looks aren't everything." He grabbed her hand and kissed the back of it playfully. "See? I'm still the most romantic fake husband you ever had, right?"

Callie almost didn't hear what he said. George had

already taken one step in their direction, then two. . . .

But the moment that Corey's lips brushed Callie's hand, George stopped short, a confused look crossing his face. A split second later, he spun on his heel and hurried in the opposite direction.

Callie heaved a sigh of relief. Finally turning her full attention to Corey, she smiled at him gratefully. He would never know what amazing timing he had. "Right," she agreed. "You're the king of romance. Now come on, let's get back to work. It's almost time for the bell."

Carole's father was waiting for her when she got home from school that day. "Honey," Colonel Hanson said, leading the way into their bright, cozy kitchen, "sit down for a minute. I want to talk to you."

Carole sank into her usual chair at the pine table and glanced at him, wondering what was going on. "Sure, Dad," she said. "What's up?"

Colonel Hanson sat down across from her and folded his hands in front of him. He smiled at her. "So, how did everyone react today when you told them your scores?"

For a second Carole wasn't even sure what he was talking about. Then she remembered. The PSATs. "Oh," she said. "Um, Lisa was really impressed."

That much was true. Apparently, almost all the

juniors had received their scores the day before, and Lisa had heard about it. She'd sought out Carole right after homeroom to ask how she'd done. Her expression had been cautiously sympathetic at first, as though she was expecting to have to console Carole on doing poorly. But when Carole had mentioned her score, Lisa's eyes had widened and she'd looked downright shocked. "Wow," she'd said slowly. "That's forty points higher than my score last year."

"Yes, I'm sure she was," Colonel Hanson said. "Lisa's a smart girl. She knows what wonderful news this is for your future." He sighed happily. "Anyway, how did your friends do? Did Stevie get her scores back?"

"I don't know." Carole shrugged. "I'm grounded, remember? And I guess I didn't think to ask Lisa if she'd talked to her."

"Ah, yes." Colonel Hanson stroked his chin thoughtfully. "The grounding. That's the other thing I wanted to talk to you about, honey."

"What about it?" Carole felt a pang of concern. Now that her father was so gung ho about the PSATs, was he going to insist that she spend even more time on her homework? Maybe he would even make her give up working with Hometown Hope.

"I've been thinking about your punishment," her father said, leaning forward and gazing at her somberly. "I really want you to understand that what

91

you did—cheating on that test, then lying about it—was very, very wrong."

Carole nodded. "I know, Dad," she said. "But listen, I've really been trying to keep up in school since then, and I—"

"Wait." Colonel Hanson held up a hand, interrupting her. "Just let me finish, honey. I was about to say that, after our little talk the other day, I think you really do understand your responsibility in this matter. And that's a good thing."

Carole nodded silently. *What's this all about?* she wondered, wishing that her father would just get to the point.

"I still believe that you need to be punished for your mistake," Colonel Hanson went on. "However, I also think you deserve a reward for your excellent scores on the PSATs."

"A reward?" Carole repeated.

Colonel Hanson nodded. "That's why I've decided to compromise by adjusting your grounding slightly." He took a deep breath and smiled. "From now on, I'm going to let you go back to spending some time at Pine Hollow."

Carole gasped. "Wha—?" she sputtered, feeling as though she'd just fallen off the planet into some new, unbelievable world where all her dreams came true. Was she hearing things? Or had her father just said she could go back to riding? "I—wha—"

Before she could spit out anything coherent, her

father held up his hand again. "Just a minute," he said seriously. "This doesn't mean you can go back to your old schedule. For one thing, you're still technically grounded. No hanging out at TD's with your friends, no unnecessary phone calls."

"But what about Pine Hollow?" Carole choked out, her head whirling like a merry-go-round out of control. "I can go back to riding?"

"Well, as I said, not on your old schedule." Her father held up a finger. "For one thing, I still don't want you going back to that job yet. And I don't want you at the stable every day. We'll say four days a week for now, and no more than two hours per day."

That was nowhere near the four or five hours Carole had spent at the stable almost every weekday before her grounding, let alone the ten plus she'd put in on Saturdays, Sundays, and holidays. But it still seemed like a miracle. Jumping out of her chair, she raced around the table and wrapped her arms around her father. "Thank you, Dad!" she mumbled into his neck. "Thank you so much!"

Colonel Hanson turned in his chair and hugged her back. "Don't thank me," he said. "Thank yourself, for taking that test seriously enough to do so well."

Carole didn't answer. Why worry about the reasons he was letting her off the hook? The only important thing was that she could go back to Pine Hollow now, without having to survive through several more endless, dreary weeks without riding. It was so unbelievable and wonderful that she reached down and surreptitiously pinched herself on the leg, just to make sure she wasn't going to wake up and discover it was all a dream.

Pulling back, she planted a kiss on her father's forehead. "Well, thanks anyway," she said. "For being such a great dad. So when does this new arrangement start, exactly?"

"Right now, if you like." Colonel Hanson smiled. "Go ahead. But remember—two hours. That's it."

"Two hours," Carole repeated eagerly, already heading for the kitchen door. "Got it. See you in two hours."

She raced upstairs and started digging out her riding gear. *I can't wait to tell my friends the news!* she thought as she started peeling off her school clothes. *I hope Lisa and Stevie are there today. Callie and the guys, too. They'll be so surprised. So will Max and Red and Denise and Ben—*

She stopped with one leg in her breeches. Ben. Whether or not her other friends were at the stable when she arrived, she could pretty much count on Ben's being there. Her stomach flipped at the thought of seeing him again so soon.

But that wasn't the strangest part. The strangest part was that she wasn't quite sure whether her reaction was due to nervousness—or anticipation.

SEVEN

Stevie glanced at her watch and groaned. "Spike!" she said sharply. "Enough with the drum solo, okay? It's getting late."

Spike abruptly stopped hammering his spoon on the table of their booth at TD's and rolled his eyes dramatically. "Nag, nag, nag," he said. "That's all you ever do. Why'd I ever decide to get married in the first place?"

"You got me," Stevie snapped. She jabbed her pen at the notebook on the table between them, almost spilling her root beer float in the process. "Can we focus here, please?"

As Spike shrugged and glanced at the notebook, Stevie checked her watch again. She was supposed to meet Phil in less than an hour, and she didn't want to be late. They hadn't been out on a real date, just the two of them, since before the party that had resulted in Stevie's grounding.

"All right," she said briskly, pulling the notebook back from Spike. "Now, we've got to get this budget done—unless you want a repeat of this afternoon's marriage class, that is."

Spike laughed. "Yeah, that was pretty funny, wasn't it?" he said complacently, picking up his spoon again and tapping it against his sundae dish.

Stevie scowled at him. Spike might have thought it was hysterical to have everyone laugh at their wedding vows, but she hadn't been nearly so amused. Her "husband" had stood up in the middle of her improvised vows and dramatically promised to have "only twelve or thirteen affairs a month."

"It was a laugh riot," she muttered, glaring at him. Reaching across the table, she grabbed his spoon and tossed it onto the next table, which was empty.

"Hey!" he protested, leaning over to retrieve it. "I'm not done with my ice cream yet." He dug into his half-melted sundae and made a big production of smacking his lips appreciatively. "Mmmm, that's the stuff," he mumbled through a mouthful of ice cream and hot fudge.

Stevie chose to ignore that. "So anyway," she said, glancing at the notebook, "I've already written down a list of stuff we'll need to include in the budget. Rent or mortgage payments, car insurance, gas, groceries . . ."

"Don't forget beer," Spike broke in. "I'll need at least six cases a month. More when I have the guys over for poker."

"Whatever," Stevie said irritably. "If you'd just be serious about this for ten seconds, we could finish and then we could both go home."

Spike shrugged and licked his spoon. "Okay, okay," he said. "I'm serious now. Totally serious. Let me see that." He grabbed the notebook and Stevie's pen. "Okay, I see a few things you forgot."

He scribbled for a few minutes, hiding what he was doing with his other arm. Stevie watched suspiciously. "What are you writing?"

"You'll see." Spike jotted a few last words, then handed the notebook back to her. "Check it out. The perfect budget."

Stevie glanced at what he'd written. Beneath the list she'd made, he had written just three things:

> *Beer*
> *More beer*
> *Oh yeah, and don't forget the beer*

Stevie felt like throwing the notebook at him, but she gritted her teeth and did her best to control her temper. *He's just trying to bug you,* she reminded herself. *Chill, and maybe he'll get bored.* She glared at him. He was grinning back at her, looking very proud of himself and tapping his water glass with his spoon. *And if not,* Stevie added, *then you'll just have to kill him.*

That reminded her of another item she'd forgotten

to include in her budget. Yanking her pen out of Spike's hand, she wrote LIFE INSURANCE in large letters at the top of the list.

"Look," she told Spike grimly. "I don't want to be here any more than you do. But marriage class is first period tomorrow, so if we don't get this done now, we—" She broke off in midsentence as she spotted Veronica diAngelo and Zach Lincoln entering the restaurant.

Aha! she thought excitedly. She'd been trying to find out how Veronica and Zach were doing on the project all day. But when she'd tried to talk to Veronica during gym class, Ms. Monroe had gotten annoyed and made her run laps. At lunch, after talking with Callie, she'd approached Zach. But he'd been sitting with a bunch of his geeky friends, and all she could get out of him before the bell rang was that he'd never actually marry anyone who thought *Titanic* was a better movie than *Star Wars*. And after the wedding vow fiasco in marriage class, she hadn't been in the mood to do anything but slink away as quickly as she could when Miss Fenton released them.

But this could be her big chance to nail down some quotes for her story. "Here," she said distractedly, shoving the notebook toward Spike again. "Marriage is all about teamwork, right? Well, I did my part of the budget. So you can finish it. For real this time. I'll be back in a minute."

Without waiting for an answer, she got up and hurried across the restaurant toward Veronica and Zach, who were just taking a seat at a booth on the opposite wall. Zach glanced up at her approach.

"Oh," he said flatly, the tic over his left eye jerking at his eyelid. "Stevie. It's you again."

"Hi, Zach." Stevie greeted him with her best smile. "How's it going?"

Veronica looked startled to see her. "Stevie?" she snapped. "What in the world are *you* doing here?"

"Uh, gee, let me think about that one." Stevie put a finger to her chin and pretended to ponder the question. "Eating ice cream?"

Veronica tossed her long, smooth dark hair over her shoulder. "Duh," she said. "What I meant was, no one cool has come here since, like, eighth grade."

Stevie hid a smile. *That explains why they're here,* she thought. *Veronica would never go anyplace she actually thought was cool. Otherwise, some of her cool friends might see her with Blinkin' Lincoln.*

"So I guess you guys are here working on your budget, huh?" Stevie said innocently, leaning against the edge of their booth. "How's that going so far?"

"What do you care?" Veronica snapped. "Now if you don't mind, we're busy."

Stevie smiled sweetly. She wasn't about to let Veronica's obnoxious comments get to her. Not when she had a story to do. "I know," she said, glancing at Zach with an even bigger smile. "This marriage

99

project is turning out to be more work than we thought, huh?"

Zach shrugged his angular shoulders. "Then why are you looking so happy about it?" he asked bluntly.

"Oh, I just think it's really interesting," Stevie replied smoothly, taking her grin down a notch. She'd forgotten how truly weird Zach actually was. People had always given him a hard time because of the tic above his eye, but she suspected that his personality would have been enough to make him an outcast even without that. "Um, I mean, it's fascinating to see the teamwork that can happen between two people with such different backgrounds. What do you think?"

Veronica stared at her suspiciously. "Why do you care what we think?" she said. "Mind your own business."

"Yeah, you'd better watch it, Stevie," Zach put in. "My dear wife isn't very friendly, you know. Sort of like a lifetime companion and a vicious guard dog rolled into one."

Veronica snorted, looking more irritated than angry at Zach's comment. "That's funny, coming from someone who could scare all kinds of pets away just by looking at them."

The waitress appeared at that moment with two glasses of water. "Oh," she said when she saw Stevie. "Are there going to be three of you?"

"No," Veronica said icily, "there aren't."

The waitress shrugged. "Okay. Are you ready to order?"

"We'll need a minute," Veronica replied curtly before Zach could say a word. "We'll call you when we're ready."

The waitress raised an eyebrow at Veronica's imperious tone. She shrugged again and turned away.

"So anyway," Stevie said brightly, deciding the conversation had veered a little too far off the topic, "back to the project. I thought your vows were very interesting. Very poetic. Whose idea was that stuff about walking together through the garden of life?"

Veronica shrugged and wiped the edge of her water glass with her napkin. "If you must know, those were the vows my sappy cousin wrote for her wedding last spring. I figured Miss Fenton would lap that stuff up."

"Really?" Stevie pricked up her ears at that. "Plagiarizing vows? Doesn't sound like such a hot way to start off a lifetime of bliss to me. I'm sure my readers are going to be very interested in that."

"Readers?" Veronica asked quickly. "What readers? What are you talking about?"

Stevie winced. She hadn't meant to let Veronica know that she was writing about her for the *Sentinel*. "Um, nothing," she said quickly, wishing she'd kept her big mouth shut.

Veronica narrowed her eyes skeptically. "Come on. Spill," she said. "What are you up to? I should've wondered that from the start. It's not like you're usually dying to stop by and chat."

"Okay, fine." Stevie gave in. Veronica might be obnoxious, but she wasn't stupid. Now that her suspicions were raised, she wasn't likely to give up until she figured out the truth. "I guess you might as well know. I'm planning to feature the two of you in my article about the marriage project." She waved an arm to include Zach. "You're going to be one of the three couples I use to illustrate what the project's all about."

"Are you clinical?" Veronica demanded furiously. "You can't write about me in some stupid newspaper article. I never gave you permission for that."

Stevie snorted. Maybe Veronica wasn't stupid, but sometimes she could be so clueless that it was downright laughable. "No kidding," she said. "Do you think Woodward and Bernstein got permission from everyone they were writing about before their story broke?"

"What?" Veronica scowled. "Who cares about your geeky newspaper friends? I just want you to promise you won't write a single word about me."

"Fat chance." Deciding that the moment for undercover reporting was way past, Stevie whipped her small notebook out of her jeans pocket. "So Zach, do you want to go on record with any comments about your partnership with Veronica so far?"

Zach glanced up from his straw wrapper, which he

seemed to be fashioning into some kind of animal. "Sure," he said immediately. "I want the world to know that I was forced into this marriage against my will. It's spouse abuse, I tell you. Besides, I would never marry someone like her." He jerked his head toward Veronica, his tic dancing wildly and his small brown eyes gleaming with mischief. Or was it malice? Stevie couldn't tell. "She's way too shallow. She wants to spend our entire budget on designer clothes and manicures."

"Shut up!" Veronica whirled toward her husband with fury in her eyes. "Don't egg her on, you idiot. She'll probably actually print that stuff in the paper, you know!"

Zach shrugged and sipped his water calmly. "The truth will come out, and I shall be hailed as a martyr of my gender. And my species."

Veronica just stared at Zach for a moment, looking as though she wanted to throttle him right then and there. Instead, she turned on Stevie. "Look," she said vehemently. "Consider this a warning, okay? If you print one word about me in your pathetic little article, you'll be sorry."

Stevie grinned. *This is even better than I thought,* she gloated silently. *Veronica's obnoxiousness is bringing out Zach's inner weirdo, and vice versa. It's the perfect vicious circle, with the emphasis on* vicious. *And it's going to make great reading!*

"A good journalist never lets threats and intimidation stop her," she said, vaguely recalling a line she'd heard in a movie or somewhere. "We still have a little thing called freedom of the press in this country, remember?"

On that note, she turned and hurried away. Behind her, she could hear Veronica berating Zach for speaking up. Stevie grinned. This was going to be fun.

When she reached their booth, Spike was just climbing to his feet. "Yo," he said. "I've got to roll. But don't worry—I finished the budget."

"Really?" Stevie frowned. "You mean, you actually did it right? As in, you allotted money for something other than beer?"

"Uh-huh. I swear. I worked in all the essentials." Spike shrugged. "It's not so hard, really—just prioritizing. Right?"

"Right," Stevie replied cautiously. The guest speaker that day, a financial adviser, had spent a lot of time talking about prioritizing. Stevie was a little amazed that Spike had been paying enough attention to pick up on that. "Well, okay. Let me see it."

"No, no!" Spike slid the notebook behind his back and waggled one finger playfully in her face. "Come on. We're married, remember? We've got to trust each other. And trust me, the budget is totally done."

Stevie shrugged impatiently. She didn't have time to stand around playing games with Spike. For one thing, she wanted to get home and make a few notes for her article while her little chat with Zach and Veronica was fresh in her mind. If she left now, she would have just enough time to do that and run a brush through her hair before it was time to go and meet Phil.

"Fine," she told Spike, glad that he'd apparently made himself useful for once. "Thanks. See you tomorrow."

"What about the phone bill?" Callie asked, leaning closer to study the sheets that Corey had set out on the wooden mounting block.

Corey smacked himself on the forehead. "Darn! I knew I was going to forget something." He smiled sheepishly and punched a few numbers into the calculator he'd brought. "Sorry about that."

"Don't apologize!" Callie exclaimed. "I mean, please. You practically did the whole assignment yourself before you even got here."

"It was no big deal. I had a study hall today." Corey studied the numbers on the calculator and then started adjusting some of the figures in the chart he'd made.

Meanwhile, Callie glanced around the indoor ring. She'd asked Corey to meet her at Pine Hollow to work on their budget, since the hours of daylight she had for riding were getting shorter and she didn't want to waste a minute. The beginning riding class was out on the trails with Red O'Malley, and there were no other lessons scheduled that day as far as she knew, so she hoped they'd have the ring to themselves long enough to get their assignment finished.

"There," Corey said after a moment, nodding with satisfaction. "I think that should do it. We managed to allot enough funds for all the necessities—including a working phone—plus a decent amount for savings. And we still have enough left over for fun. How about a Caribbean vacation?"

Callie smiled. "Sounds good to me," she said. "I'm sure Jamaica's nice this time of year." She sneaked a peek at her watch, estimating how long it would take her to tack up Barq and set up some cavalletti in the schooling ring.

"Got a date?" Corey joked.

Callie blushed, realizing her time check hadn't been quite as subtle as she'd intended. "Sort of," she replied. "With a horse."

"Well, I guess a husband can't really be jealous of that." Corey grinned and tucked his pen and calculator back in his backpack. "Anyway, I think we're all set for today. I'd better take off and leave you to your hundred-mile ride or whatever."

Callie nodded and smiled gratefully. "Thanks. And thanks again for doing all that extra work in your study hall. Come on, I'll walk you out."

Corey finished packing his things away, then the two of them headed toward the entrance of the indoor ring. The wide wooden doors were propped open, and they paused in the doorway. "Okay, then," Corey said cheerfully. "I guess I'll see you tomor—"

"Callie?" a new voice interrupted. "What are you doing in there?"

Callie glanced across the stable entryway. George had just emerged from the stable aisle with his mare, Joyride, in tow. He was frowning at her and Corey.

Biting back a sigh, Callie forced a smile. "Hi, George," she said. "You know Corey, right?" The two guys didn't run in the same crowd—actually, George didn't run with any crowd, as far as Callie could tell—but Fenton Hall was a fairly small school. Almost everyone there knew just about everyone else, by sight at least.

George shrugged. "Sure," he said, staring rather suspiciously at the other guy. "I just didn't know he was a rider."

"I'm not," Corey said easily, giving George a friendly smile. "But it just so happens I've married a woman who spends all her time at the stable."

"Callie is a great rider," George agreed quickly. "She's won all kinds of endurance races, and Max says she has great balance. Everyone at Pine Hollow thinks she's amazing. We're all really proud of her."

Callie shot Corey a quick glance, feeling a little embarrassed by George's gushing. She didn't want Corey to think they were close friends, let alone anything more—though that seemed to be exactly the impression George was trying to project.

107

George wasn't finished. "It's a good thing this marriage project is just fake, anyway," he said. "Because in real life, Callie would never, ever be interested in any guy who wasn't a rider."

Callie's jaw dropped. She was so taken aback by George's statement that she couldn't respond for a second. Where did he get off telling people who she would or wouldn't date? In truth, only a few of the guys Callie had dated in her old hometown had been riders.

But that's not even the point, Callie reminded herself. Her initial surprise was passing, being replaced by bubbling anger. *The point is, he's acting like he knows everything about me. Almost like he owns me or something.*

"Well, anyway," Corey said, obviously doing his best to smooth over the awkward moment, "I guess there are lots of odd couples working together for this project. That's what happens when you go by computer dating." He chuckled politely at his own joke. George just stared at him blankly, and Callie clenched her fists, wishing George would go away and leave her alone. For good.

Fortunately, an interruption arrived in the form of Rachel Hart, who emerged from the other stable aisle. The intermediate rider was leading Carole's horse, Starlight, who was fully tacked up.

"Oh!" Rachel said when she saw them all standing there. "Sorry. I thought the ring was free."

"It is," Callie called hastily. "Come on in. Corey and I were just leaving." She pointedly ignored George, who was still hovering in the entryway with Joyride. His horse was stomping her front hooves impatiently and obviously wondering what the holdup was.

"Yeah, I'd better motor," Corey told Callie as Rachel led Starlight past them. "My girlfriend's expecting me." With a quick wave, he headed for the exit.

For a fleeting moment, Callie wished that Corey hadn't mentioned his girlfriend in front of George. But soon the feeling passed, and she shook her head, a little annoyed with herself. The situation with George was really getting ridiculous. Why couldn't she make him understand that she wasn't ever going to be interested in him?

George watched the other guy until he'd disappeared through the stable doors, then turned to smile uncertainly at Callie. "Well, now that he's gone, I guess you can finally get tacked up, huh?" he asked, sounding as cheerful as ever.

"I guess," Callie said shortly. She still felt angry with him, though the feeling was passing. Her mind was already turning toward her coming session with Barq. There was a lot she wanted to accomplish this week, and she couldn't afford to waste a single minute worrying about George.

George cleared his throat. "Er, actually, I was

thinking of taking a nice long trail ride this afternoon." He smiled at her hopefully and gestured at his mare. "Joy could use a change of pace—we've been spending a lot of time in the ring. Need some company while you train?"

"No thanks," Callie said bluntly. "All I'm going to be doing is working Barq over cavalletti for the next hour in the schooling ring. So you might as well just go ahead on your trail ride."

She turned and hurried toward Barq's stall before George could answer. She didn't have time to deal with his fragile ego at the moment. She had work to do.

EIGHT

Carole pushed open the wide wooden door and just stood stock-still for a moment, letting the glorious, familiar, intoxicating smell of horses wash over her. *I can't believe it*, she thought, tears of pure happiness prickling the corners of her eyes. *I can't believe I'm really here.*

"Yo!" Max's voice drifted toward her from somewhere down the stable aisle. "Whoever's out there, shut the door. You're letting the cold air in."

"Sorry." Carole quickly stepped inside and pulled the door closed behind her. Blinking back her tears, she took another deep breath.

"Carole?" Max's surprised voice was soon followed by Max himself as he hurried into the entryway, looking wary. "What are you doing here?"

"Don't worry," Carole assured him. "It's okay. Dad said I could come." She quickly explained the situation and her father's new rules.

"Oh!" Max looked relieved. "Well, I suppose congratulations are in order on your scores."

"Thanks." Carole still felt a little uncomfortable when she thought about that. Yes, she'd studied for the standardized test. She and all her friends had studied together. But she didn't quite feel like she deserved all the hubbub about her great score. After all, if star student Lisa had actually gotten a lower score than she had, didn't that prove that the PSATs were really kind of bogus?

"I'm sorry to hear you won't be coming back to work yet, though." Max smiled ruefully. "I've been looking high and low for a decent stable hand to hire, but it hasn't been quite as easy to find someone as I'd hoped."

"Really?" Carole appreciated that Max was being open with her about trying to hire someone to handle her workload. He'd assured her when she'd quit that she would always have a job at Pine Hollow, and she knew he meant it. But that didn't stop her from feeling guilty about leaving him in the lurch. "Um, I'm sorry to hear that."

Max waved one hand dismissively. "Don't worry, it's not as bad as all that," he assured her. "Like I said, it's been more challenging that I expected. But I've seen one or two promising candidates so far, and another's coming by later this week." Max shrugged. "I should have someone here by New Year's, if not before."

Carole nodded. New Year's was the original end of her banishment from the stable. But she wasn't sure if that meant she would be free to take her job back at that time. She'd been afraid to press her father for too many details. "That's good," she said. "Um, so how is everything around here?"

"Just fine." Max smiled at her. "But don't feel you have to stand around here making small talk with me, Carole. I know you're eager to go see Starlight. He's in the indoor ring with Rachel."

Carole nodded, feeling a twinge of disappointment. If Rachel Hart was already working with Starlight, that meant Carole wouldn't have a chance to ride him that day after all. Carole had arranged with the younger girl to take over Starlight's exercise and care while she was grounded. It was a good deal for both of them, since Carole knew that her horse would be getting plenty of attention and Rachel wanted to prove to her parents that she was ready to have a horse of her own.

Still, knowing that she would have to wait one more day to ride her horse dampened Carole's happiness only a little bit. It was good just to be back at the stable where she belonged.

The faint sound of a ringing phone came down the hall. "Oops, I'd better get that. It may be someone calling about the job." Max started to hurry off in the direction of the office, then paused and glanced at Carole over his shoulder. "And by the way, welcome back."

"Thanks," Carole said with feeling. "It's great to be back."

She turned and hurried across the entryway toward the indoor ring. The wooden doors were almost closed, but as she approached, she could hear the sound of hoofbeats from inside. Smiling with anticipation, she pushed open one of the doors.

"Surprise!" she called as she spotted Rachel trotting across the ring. Starlight looked wonderful. His mahogany coat was glossy, and his eyes were bright. "Guess who's—"

She stopped short as she realized, belatedly, that Rachel and Starlight weren't alone. Ben Marlow was standing off to one side, watching Starlight critically.

Carole felt her face turning bright red. She'd known she was certain to run into Ben at the stable that day. But still, she wasn't prepared for how she felt now that she was actually standing there looking at him.

He met her gaze for a second before turning his attention back to the horse. Carole blushed even deeper. With an effort, she dragged her gaze away from Ben and smiled at Rachel, who was riding toward her with a delighted smile on her small, pretty face.

"Hi!" Rachel called breathlessly, pulling Starlight to a stop and sliding out of the saddle, landing lightly on her feet and leading him forward. "What are you doing here? I thought you couldn't come back until January."

"So did I," Carole said, doing her best to sound

natural. She carefully kept her eyes on Rachel and Starlight. The gelding stretched his neck forward, snuffling at her curiously. He let out a snort as she stroked his soft nose. "But my dad gave me an early reprieve. Sort of, anyway. I can come to the stable four times a week." Suddenly realizing that her change of plans would affect Rachel, she added, "But don't worry. I still need for you to keep helping me out with Starlight. If you want to, I mean."

"Of course I do!" Rachel beamed and patted Starlight on the neck. "He's an amazing horse. Totally amazing and wonderful. I'm learning so much from him every single day!" Rachel was usually on the quiet side, but she was chattering excitedly now. Carole guessed that Starlight had something to do with that, and she understood the feeling perfectly.

She forced herself to smile at the younger girl and tried not to notice that Ben was edging toward the door as they spoke. "That's good. He's always been a great teacher for me, too."

"Of course, he's not the only one who's been teaching me a lot," Rachel added, turning and gesturing at Ben. "Ben's been great, too. I was a little nervous at first about all the responsibility—I definitely didn't want to do anything wrong while I was taking care of Starlight." She shrugged and grinned happily at Ben. "But then Ben started helping me, and that made me feel so much better. He's been totally amazing."

The young stable hand stopped dead in his tracks, looking like a trapped animal that was seriously thinking about gnawing off its own leg to escape. "Uh, no big deal," he mumbled uncertainly.

Carole felt flustered. *What's going on here?* she wondered. *It's not like Ben to play baby-sitter to the younger riders. I mean, most of them are scared to death of him. So why is he taking an interest now? Does this have something to do with before, when he kept implying that I wasn't paying enough attention to Starlight? Is he still worried about him?*

She bit her lip, thinking back over a few of Ben's cryptic comments from the past couple of months. For a while, Carole had become very involved in training another horse, Samson. During that time, Ben had let her know more than once that he'd noticed she was spending more time with Samson and less with Starlight. Eventually Samson had left Pine Hollow, which Carole supposed meant Ben would have to let up on her about Starlight. But the two of them had never really talked about the issue.

Big surprise there, Carole thought sarcastically. *When was the last time Ben and I ever really talked about anything? Or the first, for that matter?*

"Ben?" Rachel said uncertainly. "Where are you going?"

Carole saw that Ben was moving toward the door again. He shrugged, not meeting anyone's eye.

"Chores," he muttered. "Lots to do." With that, he spun and hurried toward the door, disappearing through it without another word.

Rachel stared after him in astonishment. "What was that all about?" she said plaintively. "He said he could stay as long as I needed today. He was going to help me with my half-pass."

Carole was pretty sure she knew the reason for Ben's sudden change of plans. He didn't want to be in the same room with her. Doing her best to hide her humiliation, she shrugged. "Um, I don't know. But I can help you out with your half-pass if you want."

"Oh! Don't be silly." Rachel smiled and held out Starlight's reins. "You should ride him."

"No, no," Carole protested hastily. "You go ahead. I don't want to interrupt your session."

Rachel shook her head firmly. "You ride him. That's what you came for, right? And he is your horse."

Carole hesitated. She wanted to do the right thing and insist more firmly that the younger girl finish her session. But she couldn't resist. "Well, okay," she said at last, accepting the reins with a grateful smile. "Thanks."

"Sure." Rachel smiled. "Want a leg up?"

Carole nodded. Suddenly she couldn't wait to get back in the saddle—not even long enough to lead Starlight across the ring to the mounting block. She gave Starlight a pat, gathered the reins, and got into position on his left side.

Rachel held out her hands and Carole launched herself upward. Settling down into the saddle, feeling Starlight's warm bulk beneath her, she let out a sigh of sheer joy.

"Come on, boy," she whispered, hardly noticing as Rachel waved and left the ring. She tightened up on the reins and signaled for a trot. "Let's ride!"

Lisa had just finished checking over her calculus problems when the phone rang in the hall outside her room. Dropping her pencil on the desk, she hopped up and hurried to answer, knowing there was little chance her mother was going to get it. Mrs. Atwood was exactly where she'd been most of the time for the past three days—on the couch in the living room, wrapped in her fluffiest bathrobe, with a bag of cookies and a glass of wine on the coffee table in front of her and some weepy old romance playing on the VCR.

I guess I should get used to it, Lisa thought grimly as she grabbed the receiver just before the answering machine clicked on. *I already know from the divorce that Mom's not too great at dealing with breakups.*

"Hello?" she said into the phone. "Atwood residence."

"Yo!" Stevie's familiar voice greeted her. "It's me."

"Hi. How was your date with Phil?" Lisa asked,

though she could already guess from Stevie's buoyant tone that it had gone well. "Where did you guys go?"

"It was great! We didn't go anywhere special; just hung out."

Stevie didn't elaborate, and Lisa didn't press her for details. She understood there were some moments that just didn't call for any further discussion. "That's nice," she said. "So did you tell him about your marriage project thing? Is he jealous of your new wedded bliss?"

Stevie snorted. "Yeah, right," she said. "The only thing he's worried about is how he's going to raise bail when I get picked up for murdering Spike."

Lisa laughed. "Well, at least you're getting plenty of good material for your article, right?"

"I guess. Oh! But you'll never guess what else!" Stevie exclaimed. "I stopped by Pine Hollow on my way to meet Phil, and who did I see?" She paused for dramatic effect. "Carole!"

"Really?" Lisa was surprised. "What was she doing there? She didn't sneak out behind her father's back, did she? Max won't let her get away with that."

"No, no, nothing like that," Stevie said. "The colonel let her off the hook. Well, partly, anyway. She's still not allowed to use the phone or hang out at TD's or anything like that. And she can't have her job back yet. But she's allowed to ride, like, four times a week. So she wants us all to go on a trail ride tomorrow after school to celebrate. Are you in?"

Lisa could only imagine how Carole must have reacted to that news. "Sure, sounds great," she said, playing absently with the phone cord. "Carole must be thrilled to be back, even if it's only sort of part-time by her standards. But it's not like her father to change his mind like that. What's the deal?"

"Oh, I almost forgot that part. It was because of her PSAT scores."

"Oh!" That made a lot more sense. Lisa had been startled at Carole's incredible score. In fact, for a moment she'd wondered if maybe Carole had read the numbers wrong or something.

It wouldn't be the first time she's spaced out about something like that, she thought. *And it would make more sense than the fact that Carole, who barely seems to remember to go to school most of the time, scored forty points higher on the PSATs than I did.*

Feeling a little guilty for the thought—could she actually be jealous of her best friend?—she spoke again quickly. "It's great that she did so well, isn't it?" she said to Stevie. "That reminds me. How'd you do?" She hadn't spoken with Stevie or Alex since they'd all parted ways after their trip to TD's the afternoon before.

Stevie told her. Lisa wasn't surprised by the number—it was a good, solid score, thirty points below Lisa's own but still above average. "That's great," she said sincerely. "Congratulations."

"It's about what I expected," Stevie said matter-of-factly. "But Mom and Dad were pretty pleased. And the best part is it's a whole ten points higher than Alex's score—*and* Phil's. They got the same thing."

Lisa chuckled. "I guess the men in your life are pretty consistent."

"Speaking of my academically challenged brother, he just wandered in," Stevie said. "I'll turn you over to him now—I just remembered, I need to look up some statistics about divorce rates and stuff for my article."

Before Lisa could take that in, Alex's voice replaced Stevie's in her ear. "Lisa?" he said. "Hey."

"Hey yourself," she responded, shaking off a feeling of dismay. She found herself wishing that Stevie hadn't passed the phone off to Alex so quickly. Because all of a sudden, Lisa realized she didn't know what to say to him. "Um, what's up?"

"Not much." Alex sounded as cheerful as ever. "How's my favorite girlfriend? Did you get that English paper finished last night?"

"Uh-huh." Lisa bit her lip. It was weird, but she realized she hadn't expected to see or speak to Alex at all that day. He'd had a soccer team meeting after school, and she'd planned to put in some extra work on an upcoming history project.

But that wasn't the truly weird part. The truly

weird part was that she really didn't feel like talking to him. *What happened to the days when we both used to go crazy if we couldn't be together all the time?* she wondered. *Back then, a whole day apart would have been torture. But now, it just seems like a nice break from . . .*

From what? She wasn't quite sure. From Alex? From being in a relationship?

"Lisa?" Alex said. "Are you still there? Are you okay?"

She realized she'd been silent for a long moment. "Sure," she said. "Um, I guess I'm just a little tired. Sorry."

"Oh, okay. So what are you up to tomorrow?"

"I'm not sure yet," she hedged, guessing that he hadn't heard Stevie mention the trail ride. Somehow, Lisa didn't feel like bringing it up. "What about you?"

Alex sighed noisily into the phone. "Don't ask," he said. "I have to stay after school again. My ecology teacher's showing some movie about the rain forest for extra credit, and my grade could use the boost. Plus I'll probably have to meet with Iris to do whatever ridiculous marriage homework they lay on us tomorrow. I'll tell you, this family life stuff is getting time-consuming."

Lisa smiled, feeling a little relieved. *I guess that means he can't go on the trail ride anyway. Besides, it'll be nice to spend some time with my friends—just the three of us. Or four, maybe,* she added, remembering Callie.

As she and Alex said good-bye and hung up, though, Lisa couldn't help feeling a little guilty. For not mentioning the trail ride. For being eager to get off the phone. For feeling like being back with Alex full-time was putting a strain on the rest of her life.

I guess I got used to seeing him only once in a while back when he was grounded, she thought, wandering slowly toward her room. *I thought getting back to normal would be the most amazing thing in the world. But now I'm not so sure it's working for me.*

She stopped in the middle of the hall, dismayed by the thought. What was wrong with her, anyway? She had a great, caring boyfriend who wanted to spend time with her. Most girls would kill for the kind of relationship she had with Alex.

Maybe I just need a little time to get used to being with him again, she told herself, taking another step toward her bedroom. *Or maybe this is just a normal stage in any relationship. Sort of an ebb and flow thing.*

A loud chaotic sound came from downstairs. Glancing at the stairs, Lisa heard screams and gunshots and guessed that her mother's movie had ended and she'd turned on a police show on television. Mrs. Atwood had never liked that type of program before the divorce—in fact, she'd complained loudly whenever Mr. Atwood turned one on—but these days, she'd gotten a lot less picky about what she watched.

I know one thing, anyway, Lisa told herself with a slight shudder, hurrying into her room and closing the door to shut out the sound of the TV. *Whatever weird things are going on in my head right now, I'm definitely not going to say anything about it to Alex and ruin things between us.*

NINE

"*And it's nice to see that your nose is all better, too.*" Stevie touched Phil's nose gently with her fingers.

"*Really?*" Phil replied, pulling her close. "*Then you'd better kiss it, too.*"

Stevie kissed his nose. "*And it's especially great that your chin is all better.*"

Phil tipped up his chin. "*Okay,*" he replied. "*Then you'd better kiss it, too.*"

Stevie kissed his chin, then pulled back and smiled. "*Oh, and did I mention how especially, fantastically amazing it is that your lips are so totally better?*"

"*Really?*" Phil leaned closer. "*Then you'd better—*"

"Miss Lake!" A sharp voice broke into the romantic moment. A strangely familiar voice.

Stevie's eyes flew open. She'd been so busy reliving the previous night's date with Phil that she'd completely lost track of reality. Now realizing that she was sitting in the middle of the Fenton Hall auditorium with her eyes closed and a sappy smile on her face, she felt herself blush deep crimson.

"S-Sorry," she stammered, glancing from Callie, who was sitting on her right, to Spike, sitting on her left, then back to Miss Fenton. "Um, I was just thinking about, um, relationships."

Spike smirked. "She can't stop dreaming about me," he said just loud enough for his buddies in the next row to hear.

Stevie shot him a glare that could have peeled paint as Spike's friends burst out laughing. "In your dreams, Anderson," she said icily when she could make herself heard again.

Just about the only other person who didn't look amused was Miss Fenton. She was gazing at Stevie through her bifocals with an irritated frown, her arms crossed over her chest. "All right, Miss Lake," she said. "Since you and Mr. Anderson already have our attention, perhaps you'd like to read your budget for the class. I want to get an idea of how everybody managed."

Stevie gulped. Their budget? She hadn't thought about it since leaving TD's the day before. "Where's the budget?" she hissed at Spike.

"Oh, yeah," he drawled, leaning over and grabbing a sheet of paper out of his duffel bag. "Here you go, honey."

"Thanks." Shooting him a dirty look for the *honey* part, Stevie cleared her throat and stood up. " 'Our monthly household budget, by the Andersons,' " she read. Tossing Spike another annoyed glance for that one—as if she'd ever take his name!—she read on. "'Rent: Five hundred dollars. Food and beverages: Three hundred dollars. Adult video rental: Seven thousand dollars.'"

It wasn't until the class started laughing that Stevie realized what she'd just read. "Pardon me?" Miss Fenton said, looking a bit taken aback.

"Er, sorry," Stevie said, flustered. "Um, I meant to say, videos and entertainment. Uh, and that was, uh, seventy dollars, not seven thousand." Moving on hastily, she read, "'Motorcycle fuel: Twelve million dollars.'"

This time Miss Fenton frowned. "Motorcycle fuel?" she repeated as the other students laughed again. "This project is not a joke, Miss Lake."

"Everything's a joke to *her*," Veronica diAngelo said loudly from her seat a few rows away.

Stevie felt her face turning red. Quickly scanning the rest of the budget, she saw that it only got worse. Spike had allotted money for all sorts of idiotic things, from football season passes to poker nights with his buddies. But aside from rent and food, there was no mention of any of the necessities Miss Fenton and the guest speaker had mentioned the day before.

She glared at Spike and mouthed the words *You're dead*, but he just grinned and raised his hand. "Sorry about that, Miss F," he called out. "I know our budget isn't too hot, but there's a good reason for that.

127

The little woman's not good with numbers. Think I'll have to give her a monthly allowance."

The other students howled at that, and Stevie knew she must be starting to look like an overcooked lobster. Still, as furious as she was with Spike for doing this to her, she reminded herself that she should have known better.

Why did I take his word that the budget was done? she chastised herself as Miss Fenton glared at her. Callie shot her a sympathetic glance, and everyone else continued to laugh. *Why didn't I at least read it over to myself before I opened my big mouth just now? I knew he didn't take this project seriously. I knew he'd love nothing more than to make a huge fool of me just for a laugh.*

"All right, Miss Lake," Miss Fenton said. "You might as well sit down. Now, would anyone who actually took the time to do the homework like to read their budget?"

As hands shot up here and there throughout the auditorium, Stevie sank down in her seat, relieved to be out of the spotlight. To take her mind off her almost irresistible urge to leap onto Spike and choke him until he begged for mercy, she turned her thoughts to her article. She'd spent a lot of time the night before sketching out a rough outline. But she hadn't really started writing yet; she wanted to get all the material she could before she put the words on paper. Of course, she didn't have much time—

Theresa needed a full draft of the article by Thursday afternoon at the latest if Stevie wanted to have a shot at being included in that Friday's issue.

Now I see where Deborah's coming from when she moans and groans about her tight deadlines, Stevie thought, picturing all the times Max's wife had wandered through Pine Hollow with bleary eyes and a messy ponytail after a late night of work. *I guess it's just one of the things you have to get used to when you're a journalist.*

That thought cheered her up a little bit. She liked the feeling of doing something important, like bringing information to her fellow students no matter what the cost in sleep and sweat.

Okay, so maybe describing this ridiculous project isn't exactly headline news, she thought. *But it's a start. Once Theresa sees what I can do, she's sure to give me better assignments.*

Glancing at the stage, she noticed that a portly middle-aged man had joined Miss Fenton. Stevie tuned in just in time to hear the headmistress introduce the stranger as Mr. Howe from the Fine Family Foundation.

"Hello, students," Mr. Howe said, stepping forward. He was holding a cardboard box, which he set on the podium as Miss Fenton moved back. "It's wonderful to be here, to have the opportunity to talk to you fine young people today. . . ."

Stevie let her thoughts drift away again as Mr.

Howe droned on. Once again, she tried to figure out ways she could make her article even better. She wanted it to be the best she could do—and not just to impress Theresa, either.

I can't believe I never thought of joining the school paper before this, Stevie thought. *It just seems so right for me. Like it's something I was meant to do.* She smiled as she remembered how great it had felt to open up last Friday's Washington* Reporter *and see her name there, in black and white, at the beginning of Deborah's article.* Maybe it's because I always spent so much time at the stable. Of course, if I hadn't, I probably wouldn't have noticed the problems at that retirement farm, and Deborah might have missed the story, and I might never have realized how cool being a reporter really was. . . .

She shook her head, realizing she was wasting time. Valuable time. Time she could be spending coming up with cool opening lines for her article.

I should start with something catchy, she told herself, tapping her fingers on the arm of her seat. *Maybe a famous quote, like that one about how if you get married in haste, you regret it at your leisure. Or however it goes. Who said that, anyway?* She had no idea, though she'd heard her parents use the quote once or twice about one of Stevie's older cousins. *Or maybe that's too negative. I could just start with a quote from one of my subjects. I could start with Zach saying, "I would never marry someone like her,"* and then take it from there. Or maybe—

Stevie blinked, suddenly distracted from her thoughts by the motion of a couple farther down her row getting out of their seats and walking to the front of the room. "What's going on?" she hissed to Callie.

Callie glanced at her in surprise. "What do you mean? Weren't you paying attention?"

Stevie grinned sheepishly in response. "Not exactly," she admitted.

Callie rolled her eyes. "That guy Howe brought along something he calls life lessons cards. Sounds pretty lame, but each couple has to go up there and pick one out of the box. Whatever it says is what happens next in their imaginary marriage, and they have to figure out how to deal with it."

"Oh." Stevie glanced curiously at the front of the room. The first couple was just reading their card.

"Well?" Miss Fenton asked with a smile. "What does it say, you two?"

The wife, a girl from Stevie's English lit class named Roberta, cleared her throat. " 'Your landlord raises your rent by ten percent,' " she read. She glanced at her husband and shrugged. "That doesn't sound too bad."

Mr. Howe nodded. "Who's next?" he asked, turning to Miss Fenton.

The headmistress called another pair of names,

and Stevie watched for the next few minutes as several other couples went up to the front and read their cards aloud. One card stated that the family's home was destroyed in a fire. Another pair had to deal with an elderly parent moving in with them. A third got the same raised-rent card as the first couple.

"I guess there are some repeats," Stevie commented to Callie.

Callie nodded, but before she could respond, Miss Fenton called her name. "Uh-oh," Callie whispered to Stevie as she got up. "The moment of truth." Together with Corey, who had been sitting on her other side, she hurried to the front and picked a card.

Stevie watched curiously as Corey looked at the card over Callie's shoulder. " 'Wife is transferred from her job in a small town to a higher-paying job in a large city,' " Corey read aloud. He glanced at Callie and smiled. "Congratulations, honey. Does this mean you're going to support me now?"

Callie chuckled. "We'll see," she said.

Miss Fenton shooed them offstage, then called Alex and Iris to the front. "This should be good," Stevie whispered as Callie returned to her seat. "I hope Alex's card says his house and car got blown away by a tornado."

Alex looked startled as he read his card. He glanced at Iris. "Wow," he said. "It says here we're expecting twins!"

Stevie laughed out loud. "Way to go!" she called out. "I'm going to be an aunt!"

Miss Fenton gave her a sour look. "That's enough, Miss Lake," she said. "Your turn will come soon enough." She pointed to Veronica and Zach. "Miss diAngelo and Mr. Lincoln. Come forward please and draw a card."

Veronica didn't look very happy about having to walk onstage with Zach beside her. She looked even more unhappy when she snatched the card that Zach pulled out of Mr. Howe's box and read it out loud. " 'Husband is laid off from his high-paying job,' " she read.

Stevie hooted with laughter. Most of the rest of the class giggled, too. Veronica's expensive tastes were practically legendary.

Veronica frowned, clearly not as amused as everyone else. "Whatever," she said icily, heading for her seat. "It's not like this little game really means anything, anyway."

"Wait up, dear!" Zach called loudly. "Can I borrow fifty bucks?"

Stevie was still grinning about that a few minutes later when George Wheeler and Sue Berry picked their card. It stated that George had just been diagnosed with a serious illness that would prevent him from working and require round-the-clock home care.

"Bummer for them," Stevie said sympathetically as

the couple walked down off the stage and headed back toward their seats.

"Yeah," Callie replied in a tight voice. "Major bummer."

Stevie glanced at her in surprise. But before she could comment on Callie's bitter tone, Miss Fenton called her name.

Spike stood up. "Come on," he said. "I've got a good feeling about this, honey. I bet it's going to say we won the lottery."

Stevie rolled her eyes and followed him to the stage. When Mr. Howe held out his box, she reached inside and grabbed the first card her fingers touched. Pulling it out, she scanned it quickly. *Wife is diagnosed with a serious illness*, she read. For a second she thought she'd pulled the same card as George and Iris, except that the wife was sick instead of the husband. Then she read the second line. *Her disease is treatable, but only if she moves to a faraway state to be near a specialist clinic.*

"What's it say?" Spike asked, nudging her in the shoulder and leaning over to get a look.

Stevie read the card out loud. "Looks like we're moving," she commented.

"Looks like *you're* moving," Spike corrected.

"All right, all right," Miss Fenton admonished before Stevie could respond. "That's enough, Mr. Anderson. You'll have plenty of time to discuss what you're going to do when we break into our family groups in just a few minutes."

Stevie gritted her teeth as the two of them took their seats again. Spike was wearing on her last nerve. Why did she have to get stuck with such a goof? Zach Lincoln was starting to look like an ideal husband by comparison.

When everyone had chosen a card, Miss Fenton instructed them to break into couples and start working out what they were going to do to handle their life changes. "And don't waste any time," she added. "I'll expect each couple to turn in a two-page essay tomorrow describing your plans. You might want to get started on that now."

"Ugh," Stevie mumbled as she turned to face Spike. "More homework?"

Spike shrugged and leaned over to dig through his duffel bag. "Who cares?" he said. "It's not like this is a real class or anything."

"I know," Stevie said. "But we still have to do the assignment."

"Why?" Spike sat up, a wrestling magazine in his hand. Leaning back, he propped one high-topped foot on the back of the seat in front of him, nearly kicking Lorraine Olsen in the head. "I say we just chill and deal with it tomorrow."

Stevie frowned. "Come on, get serious," she said. "We're supposed to be talking about our life cards, not hanging out. So what do you want to do about this disease clinic thing?"

"That's easy." Spike flipped open his magazine. "You're the one who's sick. So you can move off to wherever you want and get treated. That doesn't mean I have to go."

"Yes it does," Stevie argued, knocking the magazine out of his hands. "We're married, remember? We're supposed to be in this together."

Spike looked mildly irritated as he reached down to retrieve his magazine. "No way," he said. "I'm not changing *my* life."

Stevie sighed, irritated as usual by Spike's attitude. Their grades for this project might not count, but that didn't mean that Stevie wanted them to end up with the worst performance in the junior class, newspaper article or no newspaper article. But what could she do if her partner wouldn't even pretend to cooperate? As she'd said, they were in this together.

"Whatever," she muttered. "Obviously, talking to you is a huge waste of time, as usual."

She glanced at her watch. There were still fifteen minutes left in the class period. Time enough to do a little more footwork for her story.

Glancing over at Callie and Corey, who were bent over their project notebook talking earnestly, she decided they could wait. *I'll catch Callie at Pine Hollow later,* she thought. *Maybe she'll come along on our trail ride, and I can interview her then.* She glanced toward Veronica and Zach a few rows away and grinned. *Meanwhile, I might as well talk to the star-crossed lovers over there while they can't get away from each other—or from me.*

Shoving Spike's leg off the seat back, she pushed her way past him without bothering to explain where she was going. When she reached the aisle, she hurried toward Veronica and Zach. Plenty of other people were standing up and wandering around, so she was pretty sure that Miss Fenton wouldn't even notice that she wasn't with her partner.

Veronica and Zach were seated at the end of their row. When Stevie reached them, they didn't even notice for a moment—mostly because Veronica was busy yelling at her husband.

". . . and if you'd just let *me* pick the card instead of grabbing for it like a child, we wouldn't have this problem!" she exclaimed in an exasperated tone. "It's ridiculous, really. I would never marry someone who couldn't even hold down a job."

"True," Zach replied sourly. "Because any man that's idiot enough to marry *you* isn't going to want to spend any time at home. He'll take any job he can just to get out of the house."

This is great, Stevie thought gleefully. *They're the perfect opposite of Callie and Corey. This article is practically going to write itself!*

Just then Veronica glanced up and spotted her.

"Oh, great," she snapped. "It's Stevie Lake, roving reporter. What do you want now?"

"Oh, I just stopped by to see how you two are doing," Stevie said cheerfully. "Bummer about the job thing, Zach."

Zach snorted. "Get lost, Stevie," he said bluntly. "It's bad enough that I have to deal with one crazy woman. I can't handle two."

"You couldn't handle an inflatable doll, you loser," Veronica told him sharply. Whirling around to glare at Stevie, she added, "But he's right about one thing. You need to get lost. Now!"

Veronica's voice was getting pretty loud and shrill. Stevie could see other students starting to glance their way curiously. Fearing that all the commotion would attract Miss Fenton's attention, she held up her hands and pretended to give in. "Whatever. I'm going." Giving them an appeasing smile, she ambled away.

But she didn't go far. There was an empty seat in the row behind the mismatched couple, just one down from Zach. Stevie waited until Veronica and Zach were distracted by their own arguments, then ducked past the couple in the first two seats and crouched low in the empty seat. Pulling out her notebook and pen, she prepared to take notes.

Veronica was supplying plenty of material. ". . . and I don't know what there is to discuss here, anyway," she was saying to Zach. "There's just one solution. You have to go out and get another job."

"I don't know," Zach said. "I'm not sure that will be so easy. I don't want to take just *any* job, you know. There's no way I'm going to sacrifice my creative talents just to keep you in designer jeans."

"Oh, please." Veronica let out an inelegant snort. "It's not like this is real life, you know. It's just a stupid two-page essay. We're going to say that you searched the want ads and went on interviews until you found a new job that paid as well as the old one. Got it?"

"Uh-uh." Zach shook his head stubbornly. "I don't like that plan. Maybe I want to take some time off and find my true calling. I think you should go out and get a job at McDonald's so you can help support me for a change."

"What?" Veronica shrieked, sounding so incensed that Stevie couldn't quite smother her laughter.

She regretted that a second later when both of her subjects whirled around. "What are you doing back there?" Veronica shrieked. "You'd better get out of my face, Stevie Lake! Otherwise you're *really* going to be sorry!"

Stevie was about to respond when she spotted Miss Fenton heading their way, a stern look on her face. "Okay, okay," she said quickly, standing up and tucking her notebook away again. "I'm going."

Callie was hardly aware of the commotion a few rows away. She was busy jotting down notes for the essay she and Corey were already beginning to write together. It hadn't been too difficult to settle on a plan to handle their life card. Corey had quickly insisted that the best way to deal with Callie's big promotion would be for him to start looking for a job in the new city.

"It will be an adventure," he insisted. "I've always wanted to live in the big city. And it's not like we're stuck there forever. If we decide to move back to our small town later, at least we'll probably have enough money to buy a nice house there. With the big raise you're getting, we can put a lot more money into savings."

"Sounds good," Callie agreed, quickly scribbling down most of what Corey had just said. It was going to sound terrific in their essay. "Thanks for being so understanding. I'm starting realize just why I fell in love with you in the first place." She grinned.

Corey chuckled. "I know, I know. I'm a heck of a guy."

Callie smiled. She was really starting to enjoy the marriage project. Corey made the whole charade, which could have been totally lame, seem like a lot of fun.

As Corey took the notebook to read over what she'd written, Callie sat up straight to stretch out her neck and back. She was a little stiff from all the riding she'd been doing for the past couple of days. When she glanced forward to check out the clock over the stage, she noticed George. He was swiveled around in his seat two rows ahead, staring at her over the empty seats between them with a slight frown on his face.

Callie raised one eyebrow. "What's wrong, George?" she asked.

George looked embarrassed that she'd caught him staring. "Nothing," he said quickly. "Um, but I heard what, uh, *he* said." He nodded toward Corey, who glanced up curiously. "You might not be able to save that much more," he continued, his voice rather hostile. "Your cost of living will probably be a lot higher in the city than it was in the country. Didn't you think of that?"

Corey shrugged. "Actually, I hadn't. But it's a good point. Thanks, man." He tossed George a salute and bent down to make a note.

Just then George's wife spoke to him, and he turned away. Callie was relieved. "Sorry about that," she told Corey. "George can be a little, um, well . . ." She wasn't quite sure how to explain.

Corey raised one hand to stop her. "No need to apologize," he said gallantly. "A man has to expect other guys to try to move in when he's married to a wonderful woman like you, darling."

Callie laughed, relaxing immediately. "Well, I can't argue with that," she joked back. "But I'm sure plenty of girls would love to be in my shoes, too, my studly hubby."

"True, true." Corey grinned. Then he gestured at their notebook. "Anyway, I think we've pretty much

141

got an outline sketched out here for our essay. How about if we get together at lunch today and write it up? Then neither of us will have to worry about it tonight."

Callie definitely liked the sound of that. She was planning to spend the whole afternoon at Pine Hollow training. Then, once it got too dark to ride, it would be time to head home and continue her campaign to convince her parents to buy her a horse. "Sounds good," she told Corey. "Meanwhile, we've still got, like, five minutes. Let's get started now."

Corey turned to a new page in the notebook. "Okay. How should we start?" He stared into space thoughtfully for a second or two. "How about, 'It was the best of times, it was the worst of times'?"

Callie giggled. "I don't think so. How about if we just write out what our card said at the top? Then we can take it from there."

"Well, it's not quite as catchy, but . . ." Corey leaned over to copy the text from their life card.

Meanwhile, Callie noticed that George had turned around again. She looked at him with a frown. "Yes, George?" she asked, a little of her impatience creeping into her voice.

If he noticed her tone, he didn't let on. "Wow, poor you," he said in a stage whisper. He jerked his head toward Corey, who was still writing. "Too bad you got stuck with a partner who can't take anything seriously, huh?"

Corey glanced up in surprise. But Callie didn't let him say a word. "Who asked you, George?" she said sharply. "I think you'd better turn around and worry about your own essay, okay? I'll worry about mine."

George looked stunned. Bright pink spots appeared on his round cheeks, and for a moment Callie was afraid he might burst into tears.

But a second later, he turned away. He bent his head so low over his work that Callie couldn't see anything but a tuft of his wispy pale blond hair poking up over the back of the seat.

She sighed, feeling a little guilty and a lot relieved. *Enough is enough,* she thought as Corey shot her a curious glance. *It's bad enough that George can't seem to accept that we'll never be more than friends. It's worse to have to fend him off at the stable and in the halls between classes and just about everywhere else. But it's way unacceptable for him to start interrupting me when I'm in the middle of a class assignment. It's not like I want to hurt his feelings, but I'm starting to think maybe that's the only way to get through to him.*

Shaking her head, she did her best to focus on Corey and their essay again. Thankfully, George didn't turn around again for the last few minutes of the class period. And when the bell rang, he quickly gathered up his books and hurried past Callie's aisle without so much as glancing her way.

TEN

"Mom?" Lisa paused in the living room doorway. "I'm going over to Pine Hollow for a little while, okay?"

Mrs. Atwood glanced up, gathering her bathrobe more tightly around her neck. The TV was blaring so loudly that Lisa was a little surprised she'd heard her at all. "Hmmm?" she murmured, blinking fuzzily at Lisa as if wondering exactly who she was. "Oh. Fine, dear. Have a nice time."

Lisa hesitated, wishing she knew what to say to take that distracted, melancholy, haggard expression off her mother's face. But she'd been through all that before. By now she knew it was pretty hopeless to try to get through to her when she was in that state.

Instead she just sighed. "Okay, Mom," she said softly, backing away. "See you later."

She was pulling on her coat when the phone rang. For a second, Lisa was tempted to head out without answering it. But then, worried that Carole might have had a change in plans, she hurried back to the kitchen to pick it up.

"Hello?" she said breathlessly.

"Hey, sweetie," Alex's voice replied. "It's me. What are you up to?"

"Oh. Hi," Lisa said, surprised. "Uh, I was just on my way out. What are you doing? I thought you were watching some extra-credit movie after school today."

"My ecology teacher called in sick," Alex said cheerfully. "So I'm off the hook, for today at least. And Iris and I finished our marriage homework during class. So I figured I'd see if you wanted to hang out or something. Where were you headed when I called?"

"The stable," Lisa replied, feeling consternation sweep over her. She'd been looking forward to the trail ride with her friends all afternoon. It had been a long time since the three of them had been able to just hang out together. "Um, Carole's dad is letting her ride again, so Stevie and I were going to take her out on a trail ride to celebrate."

"Oh really? Sounds like fun." Alex paused, obviously waiting for an invitation.

Lisa hesitated, torn. *I should ask him to come along*, she told herself, feeling guilty for even having to think twice about it. *Stevie and Carole won't mind. And I know he missed me last week while I was away—especially since it was his first week of not being grounded.*

Still, she couldn't quite face the thought of turning the pleasant, relaxed afternoon she'd been imagining into some kind of romantic moment. "Um, I wish you could come along," she said carefully, praying that Stevie hadn't already invited her brother along. "But I think Carole wanted it to be just the three of us. You know, sort of a girl thing."

"Oh!" Alex sounded a little surprised. "Okay. Well, maybe we could get together tomorrow, then. I have practice right after school, but I could meet you at the stable afterward for a quick ride, and then we could grab some dinner or something."

"Okay," Lisa said, relieved to be off the hook for that day. "I'd better get going. See you tomorrow." As she hung up, she still felt guilty about blowing him off. But she told herself it was no big deal.

Every couple needs some time apart, she thought as she hurried toward the door. *It doesn't mean there's a problem. Not at all.*

"Thanks a million, Carole," Denise McCaskill said gratefully, watching from her seat on a trunk in the tack room as Carole finished rubbing leather conditioner into Denise's new secondhand jumping saddle. "This stupid flu bug I've got has made me so sensitive to anything the least bit smelly that I won't be able to muck out for a while."

Carole grinned at the petite, dark-haired stable manager and tossed her rag into the trash can under the sink. "Don't let Max hear you say that," she teased. "He'll be horrified."

"I know." Denise grimaced and rubbed her stomach. "Um, could you excuse me a sec?" Without waiting for an answer, she jumped up and raced out of the room. Carole heard her footsteps heading in the direction of the rest rooms at the end of the hall.

Quickly lifting Denise's saddle onto its rack, Carole stepped out into the hallway and gazed after her, worried. But at that moment she heard the clatter of boots hurrying her way. Turning, she saw Stevie and Lisa racing toward her.

"Carole!" Stevie screeched joyfully. "It's you! It's really you!"

Carole laughed out loud as Stevie raced up and flung her arms around her, almost knocking her over with her exuberant hug. "Nice to see you, too," she said, spitting out a mouthful of Stevie's dark blond hair.

Lisa grinned, reaching out and joining in to make it a three-way hug. "This is great," she said. "The three of us, just like old times."

"It hasn't been *that* long since we went on a trail ride together," Carole protested, wriggling her way free and adjusting her braid, which Stevie had knocked askew.

"It's been too long," Stevie insisted. She clapped

her hands briskly. "So come on. Let's hit that trail!" She started to go into the tack room, then stopped. "Oh, wait. Did anyone invite Callie? I meant to mention it at school, but I forgot."

"She's already out on the trail," Carole reported. "She and Barq left like fifteen minutes ago. I mentioned our trail ride, but she was pretty focused on her training."

"Oh." Stevie shrugged. "Well, then what are we waiting for?"

Carole led the way into the tack room, and soon the three of them were hurrying off to their respective horses' stalls. Carole tacked up quickly. It had been a while since she'd done it, but the motions still came automatically. "Ready to go, boy?" she murmured to Starlight, giving him a pat before leading him out of his stall.

Starlight snorted and nodded his head. Carole smiled. Max probably would have said that the horse was just shaking off a pesky fly. But Carole chose to believe otherwise.

"Me too," she whispered, pausing to plant a kiss on his big, soft nose. "Come on, let's go."

She and Starlight seemed to be the first ones ready. When Carole reached the mounting block near the outdoor schooling ring, nobody else was around. As she waited for her friends to join her, Carole couldn't help keeping a careful lookout for Ben. She hadn't seen him since that awkward moment in the indoor

148

ring the day before, but she kept expecting to run into him.

I'm sure he's here somewhere, she thought, feeling her stomach clench at the thought. *He's always here. So why haven't I seen him? Maybe he's avoiding me.*

"Here we are!" Stevie said brightly, leading Belle out of the stable building. "Where's Lisa?"

"Right behind you," Lisa called, emerging from the doorway a second later and leading Windsor. It still made Carole feel a little strange to see Lisa riding other horses—for a long time she had rarely ridden any horse but Prancer, a Thoroughbred mare who'd died just a few weeks earlier.

But she wasn't about to bring up those sad memories now. "Let's get out there," she said.

A few minutes later they were trotting across Pine Hollow's big south pasture, heading for one of their favorite wooded trails on the far side. "On the trail again," Stevie sang off-key as they rode three abreast.

As she posted automatically to Starlight's fluid trot, Carole had to resist the urge to look over her shoulder to make sure Ben wasn't lurking in the stable doorway or behind the feed shed, watching them ride away. *Stop it*, she chided herself, feeling rather foolish. *He's not back there watching you. He doesn't even seem interested in seeing you when you're at the stable, let alone when you're leaving.*

"So what's up with you two?" she asked, forcing Ben out of her mind and doing her best to focus on her friends. After all, they were the ones she'd missed the most during her grounding. And it really was awfully nice to be there with the two of them, doing what they all loved best, just as they'd been doing ever since they'd all met so many years ago. "Tell me everything."

Lisa shrugged and pulled Windsor to a walk as they reached an uphill slope. The others followed suit. "Nothing new here," Lisa said. "Um, but Stevie has really been working hard on her newspaper article. Right, Stevie?"

"Uh-huh." Stevie glanced at them. "That's one of the reasons I was asking about Callie, actually. I wanted to talk to her some more—maybe get some good quotes."

Carole nodded. The day before, Stevie had filled her in on all the details of her article. "What about Veronica?" she asked. "Is she cooperating yet?"

Stevie snorted. "Fat chance," she said. "But that doesn't matter. Veronica can't keep her big mouth shut, even when she *knows* I'm listening. I've already got plenty of material on her and Zach." At that moment Belle, sensing an opportunity, paused and lowered her head, trying to snatch a mouthful of weeds that were growing around a large boulder jutting out of the field. Stevie clucked to her horse and pulled her head up, getting the mare moving again before returning her attention to her friends. "Actually," she said then, "the only marriage that's really giving me trouble is my own. I'm even considering dropping myself from the article and just focusing on the other two couples." She grimaced. "Because right now, I'm thinking Spike and I are going to be heading for divorce court before the week is out. Some relationships just weren't meant to be."

That's for sure, Carole thought, her mind sneaking back to Ben. *If you think about it, it's pretty obvious when people are meant to be together and when they're not. Stevie and Phil knew each other for only a few days before they got together. And Lisa and Alex might have known each other a lot longer than that, but then one day they just both woke up and fell in love—bam! No question about it.*

She sighed, contrasting her friends' relationships with her own weird history with Ben. Maybe she was being an idiot even to waste so much time thinking about it. Why bother? It should be perfectly obvious that there was nothing between them. The kiss had been some kind of weird fluke.

Then why did it feel so good? Carole wondered, feeling her face turning red just thinking about that moment. *And why can't I get him out of my head, no matter how much he ignores me?*

"Carole? Carole?"

Stevie's voice broke into Carole's consciousness, and she blinked, startled. "Er, what?" she said. "Were you talking to me?"

Stevie raised one eyebrow. "Only for the past five

151

minutes," she said. "You were, like, totally out in space. So what gives? Are you bored with us already?"

Carole knew her friend was just joking, but she shook her head quickly. "No, sorry," she said. "Um, I was just thinking about something." She hesitated, glancing from Stevie to Lisa and back again. This was her chance. She still hadn't told either of her friends about kissing Ben. But now they were all here together. Now she could tell them everything.

"What is it, Carole?" Lisa asked gently. "You look kind of upset. Is something wrong?"

That was all it took. "Well, sort of," Carole said. "That is, I don't really know. What I mean is, it's about Ben."

Stevie immediately sat up a little straighter in her saddle. "Ben?" she asked, her eyes gleaming with curiosity. "What about him?"

"Um, something happened at the horse show last month, right around the time I got grounded . . . ," Carole began. The whole story came pouring out as the three of them rode through the pasture and entered the broad wooded trail beyond. The way Ben had found her hiding out, alone and upset. The concern in his dark eyes as he'd crouched down beside her. The feelings that had poured through Carole as their lips had met.

"Wow!" Stevie breathed as Carole told that part. "I can't believe he actually kissed you. Then what happened?"

"Then he ran off." Carole shrugged. "It was the horse show, and we were all so busy, so I didn't think much about it at the time. Or the fact that I barely saw him for the rest of the afternoon." She chewed on her lower lip, thinking back to that day. "Anyway, I was kind of distracted by the whole grounding thing."

Stevie nodded, steering Belle around a fallen log. "Then what?"

"So then I was sort of thinking that, you know, maybe he really liked me," Carole admitted softly. Too embarrassed at the thought to meet her friends' eyes, she kept her gaze trained on Starlight's pricked ears. "But I guess I was wrong, because when I saw him later that day, he acted like it had never happened." She took a deep breath, wanting to be completely truthful with her friends. "No, actually it was worse than that. He acted like he *wished* it had never happened."

She paused for a long moment, the sound of the horses' hooves crunching through the fallen leaves on the trail the only noise breaking the silence. *Can I tell them the rest?* Carole thought. *If I say it out loud, I can't ever take it back. . . .*

Gathering her courage, she glanced over at her friends, who were still riding beside her on the wide, smooth trail. "And that part—where he acted so, you know, *cold* about it—was the worst thing of all," she said. "Because, um, I was sort of starting to think

153

that I might, you know, possibly, sort of like him back. As more than a friend. Maybe. Or at least . . . Well, anyway. I was pretty confused. I still am, I guess."

For a second, Lisa wondered if Carole was joking. *Ben?* she thought in amazement. She was more than a little stunned by everything Carole had just said—not just the kiss, but the idea that Carole might have feelings for Ben that went beyond respect for her skill with horses. *Ben Marlow? Could Carole possibly be talking this way about the same antisocial, monosyllabic guy we all know?*

She glanced over at Stevie, who was being uncharacteristically quiet. Instead of shooting questions at Carole, she was nodding thoughtfully, seeming strangely pleased.

Now that she thought about it, Lisa realized that Stevie had been making cryptic little comments about Carole and Ben for months. *I guess she caught on a lot quicker than I did,* she thought ruefully. *I always sort of assumed that Carole was totally devoted to her job and her horses, with no time for silly stuff like crushes or boyfriends. It was, like, part of her personality. She was the one who was always the most serious about horses and riding out of the three of us. I was the one who was more serious about school. And Stevie? Well, Stevie was never very serious about anything.*

Glancing around at her friends again, Lisa realized

that Carole's interest in Ben wasn't the only thing that might have changed without her noticing. Happy-go-lucky, fun-loving Stevie really seemed to be serious about this newspaper thing. And as for Lisa herself?

Well, let's just say I might have some competition in the brains department these days, she told herself, thinking of Carole's incredible PSAT scores.

"Wow," Stevie said, finally breaking the silence. "That's really something. So what are you going to do next?"

"What can I do?" Carole asked plaintively. "Ben's still avoiding me."

"Yeah, sounds like he is acting like a jerk," Stevie admitted.

Lisa nodded, trying to imagine Ben as part of the tender, intimate moment Carole had described. It wasn't easy. "Still, he did kiss her," she reminded Stevie. "That must have meant something. Ben's not the type of guy to go around kissing girls left and right."

"True," Stevie agreed thoughtfully. "He's definitely not like most guys."

Carole sighed. "So what do you guys think I should do? Should I try to talk to him, or what?"

The trail was beginning to narrow, and Lisa steered Windsor slightly ahead of the others. "I'm not sure about that," she said over her shoulder. "It sounds like Ben's not ready to deal with this yet, and we already know he's not too great at communicating. With humans, that is." She glanced back at Carole's worried face. "And if he isn't ready, there's probably not much you can do to get him there."

Even as she spoke, Lisa wondered if she should just keep her opinions to herself. *Maybe I'm not the best person to be advising anyone else about their love life,* she thought. *After all, mine doesn't exactly seem to be in tip-top shape right now. Not if I'm lying to my boyfriend about my plans and wishing he wouldn't call me quite so often. . . .*

She shook her head as if the motion could shake those thoughts right out of her mind. This wasn't the time for that. She wanted to help Carole.

"I'm not so sure," Stevie was saying. "Maybe a nudge in the right direction is exactly what he needs. You could try to set up some kind of situation where you two end up alone again—you know, maybe out in the feed shed, mixing grain together, just the two of you. . . ."

"I don't think I want to do anything like that," Carole said, sounding doubtful. "I mean, what's the point if I have to trick him into talking to me? That's not what it's supposed to be like if we really care about each other, right? Even as friends, let alone anything more." She sighed. "Anyway, even if we ended up alone, it probably wouldn't do any good. If I can't even ask him a simple question, like who Zani

156

is, then what hope do I have for asking him about what's going on with us?"

"Zani?" Lisa repeated blankly, looking back at her friends.

Stevie nodded. "Remember? That's the little girl Carole saw with Ben last week when Hometown Hope was fixing up that park near his house."

"Oh, right." Lisa recalled Stevie telling her something about the mysterious little girl soon after her return from California.

"I'm just not sure it would be worth it," Carole said sadly. "Maybe I'm kidding myself and this is all a bunch of nothing. I just keep thinking about you guys, and what great, open, honest relationships you have with Phil and Alex. How could I ever expect to have that with someone like Ben?"

Lisa winced, thinking once again about her conversation with Alex earlier. *Stop it!* she told herself fiercely. *Just stop thinking about that. This is about Carole and Ben, not you and Alex. Besides, you didn't really lie to him. After all, if he'd come along, there's no way Carole would be spilling her guts like this. So it's all worked out just fine. Right?*

Stevie was still thinking about Carole's confession a few minutes later as they stopped to let the horses drink from the tumbling creek beside the trail, though the conversation had turned to other things at Carole's insistence. *Talk about a mixed-up relation-*

ship, she thought, patting Belle absently on the shoulder as the mare plunged her nose into the cold, rushing water. *The way Ben's been acting even makes Spike look like a real romantic.* She shuddered. *Well, okay, maybe not. . . .*

"You know, I just can't decide what to do," she commented, her mind turning back to her article. "I really like the idea of covering three couples, not just two. But if I write about myself, I'll come out looking like a total loser who can't make my marriage work. Even if it's all Spike's fault."

Before either of her friends could answer, they all heard the sound of hoofbeats coming from just beyond the next bend in the trail. A moment later Callie came into view, riding Barq.

"Hi!" Stevie called with a wave. "Fancy meeting you here."

Callie looked surprised as she pulled her horse to a stop. "Yeah," she said. "What are the odds?"

Stevie couldn't help thinking that Callie didn't look entirely thrilled to see them. "How's the training going?" she asked, wondering if Barq was giving Callie trouble.

Callie shrugged and tightened up the reins as the spirited Arabian took a few steps toward the creek. "It's okay," she said. "I've got a lot of ground to make up, though, if I want to get back to where I was before the accident."

"I'm sure Barq will be a good partner for that,"

Carole said, smiling at Callie over Starlight's broad back. "He's a really nice horse."

"Uh-huh." Callie glanced down at Barq's neck. "So what are you guys doing out here?"

"Just a little trail ride," Lisa replied. "We were going to see if you wanted to come along, but you were already gone by the time we got started."

Callie nodded. "I really wanted to get in a good, long training session today."

"Of course. We understand." Stevie smiled hopefully. "But if you have time later, I was hoping we could talk about how things are going with you and Corey. You know, for my article."

"Sure," Callie agreed, glancing distractedly at the sliver of sky showing between the treetops. "But listen, I'd better move on. I don't want to let Barq cool down too much standing around here."

"Okay. See you later," Stevie said.

"Bye." Callie urged Barq forward. The horse snorted and obeyed, with one last wistful glance at the creek. A moment later they were trotting around another curve in the trail, taking them out of sight.

"Boy, she sure seemed to be in a hurry," Carole commented, staring in the direction Callie had gone.

Stevie shrugged as she led Belle, who'd finally finished her drink, back up the gentle slope onto the trail. "She's pretty serious about this endurance stuff, I guess."

"Uh-huh," Lisa said, leading Windsor up to stand

beside Belle. She gazed at Stevie. "Just like you're serious about being a journalist, right?"

"I guess," Stevie agreed, not quite sure what Lisa was driving at.

"That's why you need to stick with your original plan and keep yourself in your article," Lisa said firmly. Ignoring Windsor, who was resting his heavy head on her shoulder and dribbling water, she kept her gaze trained on Stevie. "You need to tell the truth. That's not always easy, but it's the only way to go if you're really serious about what you're doing."

Stevie was a little startled at Lisa's assertive tone, but she had to agree that what she was saying made a lot of sense. "Okay, maybe you have a point," she admitted. "Honesty is the best policy and all that."

"Right," Lisa agreed.

Stevie glanced over at Carole for her opinion. "She's right," Carole said quietly. "I wasn't honest, and look where it got me." She glanced at her watch. "Speaking of which, I hate to say it, but we should probably head back soon. I want to have time to give Starlight a proper grooming before my two hours are up."

Soon the three of them were mounted and heading back down the trail. Lisa and Carole started chatting about Max's search for a new stable hand, but Stevie was still pondering what Lisa had said.

I guess she's right, she thought, swaying slightly as Belle moved easily along the smooth trail. *Reporting the news means telling the truth—at least as far as you know it. And that means showing all angles of a story, the embarrassing and stupid ones as well as the others.* She sighed, knowing what she had to do. *Spike and I stay in the story. For better or for worse.*

ELEVEN
11

Carole had always loved being at the stable around six or seven in the evening, when just about everyone had gone home to eat dinner, the horses were all drowsing in their stalls digesting their evening meal, and the only footsteps hurrying through the aisles belonged to the stable cats as they stalked their prey. It was such a quiet, tranquil time that Carole couldn't resist the temptation to linger, even though her friends had long since departed and her two-hour daily time limit had come and gone.

She wasn't worried about getting in trouble, though. As she was picking out Starlight's feet a little while earlier, she had suddenly remembered that her father was out of town giving a speech in Pittsburgh. He wouldn't be back until the next day and would never have to know that she'd missed her curfew just this once.

Okay, so maybe I'm not being totally honest, like Lisa kept talking about earlier, Carole thought peacefully as she moved from stall to stall, checking to make sure that each horse was settling in for the night without any problems. *And I know Dad would freak if he found out. But I'll leave soon. I just want to enjoy this for a little while longer.*

She paused outside of Rusty's stall, paying extra attention to his water bucket. Carole knew that the sorrel gelding had just been brought in that day after being turned out at pasture for the past three months in the hilly meadow near the back corner of Pine Hollow's property. A clear, cold, spring-fed pond provided water for the horses that were turned out there, and sometimes it could be hard for them to make the transition from the pond's cool, fresh water to the less natural taste of the water from the tap inside. That was why everyone at the stable always kept a close eye on pastured horses when they came in for the winter to make sure they were drinking enough.

"Poor guy," Carole murmured to the horse when she saw that the bucket was full to the brim, obviously untouched. "That stuff from the tap must taste pretty icky after what you've been drinking out there, huh?"

She gave the gelding a pat and let herself out of the stall. *Time to get out the molasses,* she thought with a smile. *Rusty always falls for that.*

After fetching the large, slightly sticky bottle of molasses that Max stored in the back of the refrigerator in the tack room for just these sorts of occasions,

Carole returned to the stall. "Here we go, buddy," she murmured, pouring a little bit of the thick, sweet substance into the bucket and stirring it with her fingers.

Rusty watched what she was doing with his ears pricked forward curiously. When Carole stepped away, wiping her hand on her jeans, the horse moved over to the bucket and sniffed at it. Seconds later, he was drinking.

Carole smiled as she screwed the cap back onto the molasses bottle. Leaving the horse to drink his fill in peace, she hurried toward the stable office, planning to leave a note so that whoever did the morning feeding would know what she'd done. That way they would know to add a slightly smaller amount of molasses each day until Rusty got used to the taste of indoor water.

She rounded the corner into the office at a swift walk, expecting it to be empty, since she hadn't heard a sound when she'd been in the tack room next door just a few minutes earlier. "Eep!" she squeaked, startled when she spotted the figure seated behind the desk.

Ben glanced up quickly, seeming just as surprised. "Oh," he said, dropping the pen he'd been using. "Uh, hi."

"Hi." Carole gulped, completely unprepared for the sudden encounter. "What are you doing?"

Ben shrugged. "Daily log," he said succinctly,

picking up his pen and jotting one last note in the thick, battered notebook on the desk in front of him.

Carole watched him, her stomach jumping like a feisty colt feeling the weight of a saddle for the first time. *You need to tell the truth*, Lisa's voice echoed inside Carole's head. *That's not always easy, but it's the only way. . . .*

Carole decided that her friend was right. Besides, she couldn't stand to have this unexpected meeting end the same way as all the others—with Ben mumbling an excuse and hurrying out, leaving Carole feeling hurt and confused. She couldn't take that again.

"Ben," she said. Her voice cracked slightly, and she cleared her throat before trying again. "Ben, can I ask you something?"

He clicked the pen shut and set it down, looking up at her warily. "Sure."

Carole took a deep breath, squeezing her hand nervously around the molasses bottle. "Um, is something wrong? I mean, are you mad at me or something? Because lately, every time you see me coming, you take off in the other direction."

She stared at the desk between them, not daring to meet his eye. Her cheeks were burning, and she really hoped she hadn't just made a huge mistake by speaking up. *Since when does that work with Ben?* she thought belatedly. *Usually it just scares him away.*

"Uh, what?" Ben said, sounding uncertain. "I'm not mad."

A little surprised that he'd answered instead of leaving, Carole dared to look at him. "Then why are you acting like you're allergic to me?" she asked softly. "I thought we were friends."

"We are," Ben replied quickly. "Er, I mean . . . Well. It's not you. Really."

Carole wasn't sure what to think of that. "What do you mean?" she asked. "I really feel like you're avoiding me, ever since, er . . ." She trailed off, not quite daring to bring up their kiss. "Well, for a while now. So what's going on?"

"It's nothing," Ben muttered, staring at his hands. Carole noticed that he was clutching the edge of the desk so hard that his knuckles were white. "Uh, I just have a lot of, you know, stuff to deal with right now."

"Does it have something to do with that little girl I saw you with?" Carole asked on a hunch. "Is this about Zani?"

Ben glanced up at her, startled. "How did you—" he began. Then he stopped himself and gulped. "Er, I mean, sort of. I guess."

"Who is she?" Carole asked, unable to hold back her curiosity any longer. What was the worst Ben could do, anyway? Leave? Refuse to answer? "Is she your little sister?"

At that, Ben let out a short, mirthless laugh. "No," he replied. "Not my sister." He heaved a sigh and pushed himself back from the desk, letting his hands fall into his lap. "Zani's my niece. She just came to stay with us. Uh, me and my granddad. Because of . . . well, . . . problems . . ."

Carole was so stunned that he'd actually answered her question that she wasn't sure what to say next. A million questions were whirling through her brain. What kind of problems did he mean? Where were the little girl's parents? How long was she staying? But just as she opened her mouth to ask some of those questions, she heard rapid footsteps hurrying down the hall outside. A second later Max burst into the office.

"Oh, hello, Ben. Carole." Max shot her a slightly suspicious look, and Carole guessed that he was probably trying to calculate how long she'd been at the stable. Luckily for her, he was distracted by something else. "Listen, has either of you seen the molasses? It's not in the tack room, and I—"

"Here it is," Carole interrupted, holding up the bottle. "I was just using it to sweeten Rusty's water."

Max looked relieved. "Great! That's exactly why I was looking for it. I noticed he wasn't drinking much earlier, and I meant to do it before dinner, but what with one thing and another . . ." He shook his head and ran one hand over his hair, a characteristic gesture when he was feeling overwhelmed. "Is it just me, or is this place twice as busy as usual these days?"

Ben stood up. "Reminds me," he said gruffly, not

really looking at either of them. "Gotta clean up the indoor ring."

He hurried out without waiting for a response. But for once, Carole wasn't too upset to see him rush off.

I still wish Ben trusted me more, she thought, waving a quick good-bye to Max before heading next door to replace the molasses bottle. *I wish he could talk to me without being practically forced to do it. And I really, really wish he would bring up that kiss.*

She blushed, as she always did when she thought about that. Brushing off her hands, she left the tack room and slowly made her way through the hushed quiet of the stable to the entryway.

Still, I guess I should try not to take it personally, she told herself. *Ben acts the way he acts because of the way he thinks the world has treated him. I should know that by now.* She shook her head, suddenly feeling a little sad. It didn't seem fair that someone as smart and talented as Ben should always have to be on the defensive. Why couldn't life be a little easier, especially for good people? *It's the whole world he's mad at, not me. I still have no idea how he really feels about me. . . .*

She sighed, pausing and glancing over her shoulder as she reached the exit. If only Max hadn't walked in . . .

But she couldn't stand around all night speculating

about maybes and might-have-beens. It was getting late. And it was long past time for her to be getting home.

Callie toyed with her slice of pumpkin pie, poking at it with her fork. She wasn't hungry—her mother's famous pepper chicken had filled her up, and then some—but she didn't want to excuse herself from the dinner table. Not until she managed to convince her parents that it was time to start shopping for a horse.

"I was thinking, maybe I could set up a few appointments for this weekend," she began, filling a brief lull in the conversation her parents were having with Scott about his latest calculus test. "I could ask Max to give me some names. He knows all the good places in the area to buy a decent horse."

Mrs. Forester sighed and shook her head, her fine-boned face drawn into a slight frown. "Really, Callie," she said. "You've spoken of nothing else for the past three days. Don't you think you ought to slow down a bit?"

"Your mother's right," Congressman Forester put in, setting down his coffee cup. "You just started riding again. It's too early to be thinking about a new horse. You need to concentrate on getting your strength back first."

Callie dropped her fork and frowned at them. "I'm working on that," she said. "But how can I really get back into competitive shape if I don't have a competitive horse to work with?"

"Frankly, sweetheart, I'm not sure that getting back into competition is what you should be most concerned with right now," her father responded sternly. "We haven't really discussed your PSAT scores. But I think you know, your mother and I had hoped you'd do a bit better than you did."

Callie rolled her eyes. *No kidding*, she thought sourly. *You wanted me to ace that stupid test so that I could follow the family tradition and go to Yale.* She didn't bother to say so out loud, though. She'd had the same argument with her parents too many times—every time she brought home a B on her report card instead of an A; every time she'd decided not to join a new club at school because she didn't want to give up any time at the stable.

She glanced at her brother, hoping for some support. After all, his SAT scores hadn't been especially brilliant, either, though he'd done reasonably well. He'd applied to Yale University, along with several other schools, but the whole family knew that the only reason he even had a shot at getting in was because of his father's occupation and family connections.

Scott kept his eyes on his plate, steadily shoveling pie into his mouth. Callie sighed noisily. "I can't believe this!" she exclaimed, returning her attention to her parents. "Are you really telling me I can't get a horse because I didn't get a high enough score on the PSATs?"

"Not at all, dear," her mother said soothingly. "We're just saying that you're in a new environment, trying to get along at a new school. . . . Don't you think it might be better for you to take it easy at the stable, perhaps focus a bit more on school for a little while?"

"No, I don't," Callie said bluntly.

"Well, we do," her father said, his voice just as firm as her own. "We want you to spend more time on your studies and maybe put in some extra work before you take the SATs."

Callie's jaw dropped. She couldn't believe what she was hearing. "Are you serious?" she cried. "But the SATs are months away! I've got to have a new horse way before then if I want to enter any races in the spring."

Her parents sighed and exchanged glances. Before either of them could say anything else, the phone rang.

"I'll get that," Congressman Forester said, dropping his napkin on the table as he stood up. "It's probably for me. Mike said he'd call if there was any word on that vote."

He hurried out of the dining room, and a second later Callie heard him pick up the phone in the kitchen. "Hello, Forester here," he said in his loud, booming voice. There was a moment's pause. "I'm sorry, but she's in the middle of eating dinner. You'll have to— What?" This time the pause was even longer. "Oh, I see. Well, just a moment, then."

He strode back into the dining room. "Callie, it's for you," he said. "Your friend George. He sounds a bit flustered—says it's urgent that he speak to you immediately."

Urgent? Callie felt a stab of worry shoot through her. What could be urgent enough to make George interrupt her dinner?

Maybe something happened at Pine Hollow, she thought anxiously as she hurried out to the kitchen to pick up the phone. *Maybe some kind of accident . . .*

"Hello?" she said breathlessly into the receiver. "George? What is it? What's wrong?"

"Hi, Callie." George sounded serious. "I'm glad you're there. I have something important to tell you."

Callie clutched the phone tighter. "What?" she asked. "Where are you, George?"

"I'm at home," George replied, sounding a bit surprised at her question. "But listen, I just found out something really horrible. You know your, uh, *friend,* Corey?" He put a little more emphasis on *friend* than seemed necessary.

"Of course," Callie said. "Why? Did something happen to him? Is he all right?"

"He's fine, I guess." George sounded a little annoyed. "But listen, I just found out that he's not who you think he is."

172

"What?" Callie wrinkled her nose, suddenly feeling as though she were a character in some kind of cheesy soap opera and that George was about to reveal that Corey was actually a nefarious international criminal or incognito rock star. She shook off the feeling, trying to stay focused. "What are you talking about, George? Get to the point."

"Well, okay." George sounded taken aback. "Um, but I should warn you, you might be shocked. Because I just found out that Corey has"—he paused and cleared his throat—"a drinking problem."

"What?" Callie let out a short laugh and collapsed against the wall behind her, caught between relief and annoyance. "Is this some kind of joke, George? Because I have to tell you, it's not very funny."

"No, no, it's true," George protested. "I just heard from a reliable source that Corey had, like, a whole bunch of beers at that party the Lakes had last month. He was throwing up the whole next day."

Callie grimaced in disbelief. Was George for real? Was this actually his idea of an emergency phone call? "Is that really why you called?" she demanded. "To tell me that?"

"I just thought you should know. As your friend, I figured I had to tell you, since Corey probably never would."

"Why should he?" Callie cried. This was just too much, especially on top of her frustrating conversation with her parents. "It's not like he's really my husband, you know. Besides, I was at that party, too. It's not like it's a big secret that people were drinking."

"I know." George sounded hurt. "But I just thought—"

"You just thought you'd interrupt my dinner with this stupid gossip?"

"It's not gossip!" George protested. "It's a warning. I thought you should know what kind of guy you've been spending so much time with lately. I was just trying to be a good friend."

Callie snorted. "Yeah, right," she said. "Well, here's a warning for you, George. Lay off with the 'friendly' warnings, okay?"

"But I just thought—" George said again.

"No!" Callie cut him off sharply. "I mean it this time. I'm starting to wonder if you're really just trying to be a good friend. Because I can't help thinking that a real friend wouldn't find so many new ways to be *annoying*!"

She slammed down the phone before he could respond. *Wow!* she thought. *That felt kind of good. It shouldn't have, but it did.*

For a moment she just stood there and stared at the phone, feeling a strange mixture of satisfaction and guilt. She knew she'd lost her temper. But hadn't George deserved it? He really seemed to have it in for Corey for some reason.

It's ridiculous, Callie thought, heading slowly back

toward the dining room. *It's as if George feels threatened by the fact that I might be friends with someone new. Like he has to put a stop to it however he can.*

She forgot all about that when she entered the dining room and saw both her parents smiling at her. "What?" she asked.

"Is everything all right with George?" her father asked.

Callie shrugged. There was really no easy answer to that one, and she didn't feel like going into it just then. "Sure," she said. "It was just, uh, a homework emergency."

Glancing over at Scott, she saw that he looked just as pleased as their parents did. He winked when he caught her gaze.

"Sit down, dear," Mrs. Forester said, gesturing to Callie's chair. "We were discussing this horse business while you were out of the room."

"That's right," Congressman Forester took over as Callie sank into her seat, wondering what was going on now. "Your brother had some interesting points to make."

"Oh, really?" Callie shot Scott a suspicious glance. He was grinning. "Like what?"

"Well, he pointed out that the accident may have had a lot to do with your troubles on the PSATs," her mother said. "Also, he seems to think that you would be able to train more efficiently if you had the right kind of horse."

175

"And that would leave more time for homework," the congressman put in.

Callie blinked, not quite sure she was following. "Yes, I suppose that's true," she said cautiously. "But what are you saying?"

Her mother beamed at her. "We're saying that you've talked us into it," she announced. "You can start looking for a new horse right away—just as long as you promise to keep up with your school-work."

Callie gasped. "Really?" she cried.

"Yes, but we still do expect you to put in some extra work before the SATs in the spring," her father said. "Your brother heard that there's an excellent test prep course over at the community college in a couple of months. If you'll agree to put aside some time for that, your mother and I will bankroll this new horse of yours."

"Thanks, Dad!" Callie exclaimed. "Thanks, Mom! I really appreciate this!" She shot Scott a grateful look. She would thank him later for helping to sway her parents' decision.

He winked at her again, obviously catching the glance and understanding what it meant. "Pretty cool, sis," he said casually. "I guess this really means you're back in the saddle, huh?"

"I guess so," Callie said, carefully keeping her voice just as casual. But inside she was singing for joy.

She picked up her fork and started stuffing pie into her mouth, afraid that if she didn't, the music would burst right out of her.

And that would be no good at all, she thought giddily. *Mom and Dad definitely won't buy me a horse if they think I've gone insane!*

. . . while some couples tied the knot only to discover that they have very different ideas about money. For instance, when Zach Lincoln suggested that his "wife," Veronica diAngelo, take a job flipping burgers, she was quick to express her dismay.

Stevie frowned at the computer screen. Somehow, that last part didn't sound quite right. She blocked off the last seven words and hit the Delete button.

"She immediately showed her anger," she muttered under her breath, trying the words on for size. "A job flipping burgers—she just about flipped out? Hmmm . . ."

She was typing that in to see how it looked when there was a knock on her bedroom door. "Stevie?" Alex's muffled voice came from outside. "Do you have a minute?"

"Not really," Stevie called back. "But come on in."

Alex opened the door and stepped inside. "Hey," he greeted her. "Working on your article?"

"Uh-huh." Stevie stared at the new sentence, reading it over a few times. Finally she decided it would do. She hit Save and then sat back in her chair and stretched, glancing at her twin brother. "Hey," she said, noticing that his expression was sort of gloomy. "What's your damage? You look weird. Is something wrong?"

Alex sighed and perched on the edge of Stevie's bed. "I don't know," he said. "Maybe. I'm not sure."

"Get to the point," Stevie ordered, leaning over to check a quote in her notebook. "I'm kind of busy here, you know."

She quickly typed a few more lines. *Zach had this to say about his wife's spending habits: "She's way too shallow," he confided to this reporter. "She wants to spend our entire budget on designer clothes and manicures."*

"I don't know." Alex let out a long, loud, dramatic sigh. "It's weird."

Stevie blinked and glanced at him again. "What?"

Alex shrugged. "Oh, I don't know. Maybe it's nothing. Probably."

"What are you babbling about?" Stevie demanded irritably. "And why are you inflicting it on me? Unless you have a point, why don't you go call Lisa and bother her for a while, okay? I have a deadline."

"Lisa." Alex's sigh was even louder and longer this time. "Actually, that's kind of what I wanted to talk to you about."

That got Stevie's attention. She saved her work again, then turned around, straddling her chair to face her brother. "What about Lisa?" she demanded, suddenly worried. "You guys didn't have another fight, did you?"

"No, nothing like that." Alex chewed on his lip and leaned back against Stevie's pillow with his hands behind his head. He stared at the ceiling. "Everything's fine. At least it seems fine. But somehow, it's weird, too."

Stevie tried not to reveal her exasperation. Her brother wasn't making much sense. She could tell that he was worried about something, though, and if it had to do with Lisa, Stevie wanted to find out more. "What's weird?" she asked as patiently as she could. "Did she say something? Is she acting different?"

Instead of answering, Alex sat up and stared at her. "What about you and Phil? Have you ever gone through a time like this?"

"A time like what?" Stevie frowned. "You still haven't told me what's wrong."

Alex rubbed his face thoughtfully, swinging one leg off the edge of the bed. "It's like I said. I don't really know," he replied. "It's sort of like we're just not connecting the way we usually do."

Stevie shrugged. "Sure, Phil and I have been through that, lots of times," she said. "Like whenever he's in a grouchy mood because he got a bad grade or got in a fight with his sisters." She grinned. "I, of course, have a perfectly wonderful temperament, so I never have that problem."

Alex seemed to have hardly heard that last part. He was shaking his head. "No, that's not what I'm talking about," he said. "I know what you mean, but that's not what this is. My mood is fine, and so is hers. But it's like ever since she got back from California, she—"

"Ah," Stevie interrupted. "So that's what this is about. You're feeling weird because you were apart for a whole week, and no offense, bro, but you've always been kind of a freak about her trips to California."

"Not this time," Alex protested. "I mean, I wasn't happy that we were apart for the whole vacation, but I was dealing with that. It was okay."

The expression in his hazel eyes was so earnest that Stevie found herself believing him. "Hmmm." She searched her mind for other examples from her relationship with Phil that might explain what Alex was feeling now. But she couldn't come up with anything. She and Phil were both pretty outspoken people—if one of them felt there was a problem brewing, they were always quick to speak up. And when they were mad at each other or upset about something, it wasn't hard to recognize. "I don't know," she said helplessly, running her hands over her dark blond hair. "To be honest, it kind of sounds like this is all in your head. Maybe you should be talking to Lisa about it, not me."

"Maybe. The trouble is, I'm not sure there's really

anything to talk about." Alex pushed himself off the bed and stood, looking dejected. "Maybe it *is* all in my head. I've never gone out with anyone for this long before—maybe this is just what it's like after a while."

"Well . . ." Stevie wasn't sure what to say to that.

Alex sighed and smiled wanly. "Anyway, thanks for listening. Sorry I interrupted your writing." He wandered out the door.

Stevie stared after him for a long moment, feeling uneasy. *That was bizarre*, she thought. *What's up with him? I thought he'd be walking on air now that he's no longer grounded and Lisa's back from her trip.*

Finally she shook her head and turned back to her computer. There was no point in sitting there worrying about them. Lisa and Alex loved each other. They would work things out somehow.

Besides, I have more important things to think about, Stevie thought. Veronica had threatened her again after school that day, warning that she'd wreak horrible revenge if Stevie so much as mentioned her name in her article. Rather than having the desired effect, that just made Stevie more determined than ever to make Veronica and Zach a large part of her story—and to make sure it was so fascinating that Theresa would absolutely have to print it. *That will teach her to try to mess with the freedom of the press,* Stevie thought with satisfaction as she began to type. *Not to mention trying to mess with Stevie Lake!*

TWELVE

"And I think our essay turned out really well," Corey commented cheerfully as he and Callie walked into the auditorium the next morning. "When I was typing it up last night, I almost believed it myself. I was ready to pull out the newspaper and start checking the city apartment listings."

"That's great. Uh, the part about the essay being good, I mean." Callie was a little distracted. She was keeping a lookout for George. It was only second period, but normally by that time she would have run into him at least a couple of times. That day, though, she hadn't seen hide nor hair of him since arriving at school, and she couldn't help wondering if he was actively avoiding her.

I hope he isn't too upset, Callie thought worriedly. *Maybe I was a little harsh on the phone last night. Not that he didn't deserve it . . .*

"Callie!" A familiar pudgy figure hopped up from a seat halfway down the auditorium aisle and rushed toward them. "There you are!"

"Hi, George," Callie greeted him cautiously. "How are you?"

George shrugged and smiled sheepishly. "Embarrassed," he said. "I acted like a real jerk, and I'm sorry. I'm really, really sorry. I just hope you can forgive me, Callie."

Callie glanced at Corey, who looked surprised. She didn't blame him. She was pretty shocked herself. "Er, what do you mean, George?" she asked uncertainly.

"You were right," George replied, clasping his hands together in front of his chest. "I was a real pest, interrupting your dinner like that. You're right, that wasn't something a good friend would do. And it wasn't my place to tell you how to deal with your project, either. Can you forgive me?"

Callie shrugged, a little embarrassed. George's voice was pretty loud, and other students were starting to turn and stare. "I guess," she said.

George turned to Corey. "I should apologize to you, too, Corey," he said earnestly. "I'm sorry if I've been getting in your face lately."

"Uh, okay." Corey looked kind of confused. "Whatever. Apology accepted, I guess."

"Good." George smiled at him, then returned his gaze to Callie. "Are we okay, then?" he asked anxiously, taking a step closer. "Still friends?"

Callie's head was spinning. Whatever kind of reaction she'd imagined George might have to their conversation the night before, this certainly wasn't it. But what could she say? He was admitting he was wrong, right?

"Um, sure, George," she said. "We're still friends."

"Great." George beamed at her. "I'm so glad."

Callie smiled back weakly, not sure what to say. Just then Miss Fenton walked onstage. "Oops! Looks like class is about to start," Callie said hastily. "Come on, Corey, we'd better find someplace to sit." She turned away from George, who was still smiling, and spotted Stevie, Alex, and Iris sitting a few rows away. Stevie saw her and waved, indicating two empty seats in their row. Relieved, Callie gestured to Corey.

Wow, Callie thought as she hurried toward the seats. *Maybe George isn't as clueless as I thought. He certainly seemed willing and able to accept that he'd stepped over the line last night. Could it be that I just haven't been clear enough after all about only wanting to be friends? Am I sending mixed signals?*

She really wasn't sure. In the past, she'd always been quick to tell off guys who didn't take no for an answer the first time, usually leaving them quivering and mortified in the scorched and melted remains of their male egos. For a while, after she'd blown away three obnoxious suitors in the space of a week, Scott had jokingly started calling her the Terminator. But George was so different from those other guys— more sensitive, almost like an eager little boy, one who could be mortally wounded by a harsh word.

She'd thought she was doing the right thing by taking it easy on him, giving him time to get over her. But by trying to spare his feelings, had she merely ended up confusing him?

She would have to think more about that later, she decided. In the meantime, she took the seat beside Stevie and glanced down the row. "Where's Spike?" she asked, noting that her friend's husband was nowhere in sight.

Stevie frowned. "Who cares?" she muttered. "There's no rule that says we have to sit together just because we were forced into this ridiculous fake marriage."

Callie raised one eyebrow, recognizing that tone. "Ooo-kay," she said, deciding to change the subject. "So how's the article going?"

"Great!" Stevie perked up immediately. "I got a lot done last night. All I need to do today is gather a few more quotes and work in whatever we cover in this class. Then it will just be a matter of proofreading and doing any last-minute revisions before my deadline this afternoon."

Corey, who had settled into the seat on Callie's other side, leaned across her and nodded. "Let me know if you want any more brilliant quotes from me, Stevie."

Stevie grinned. "I will, Corey. Thanks."

Just then Miss Fenton called for attention. A pudgy woman with pasty skin and flyaway red hair had joined her onstage. "Good morning, juniors," the headmistress said. "I'd like you to welcome Ms. Abigail Norwood. She's our guest speaker for today. She's a psychologist and author of the best-selling book *Why Some Marriages Last Forever and Some Don't.*"

Callie clapped politely along with everyone else. But she was a little distracted by George. He had moved to a seat across the aisle and a few rows ahead of her. *I've been blaming him for everything,* she thought. *But is that really fair? Maybe I've been a little uptight this week, so focused on my training and on talking to Mom and Dad about the horse thing that I haven't been as honest and understanding as I could be with George. Especially since I know very well that he isn't exactly Mr. Self-Confidence. Maybe he hasn't been playing the friend role exactly right so far, but it's not like I'm perfect, either.*

She wasn't sure what to think about that idea. But soon the thought of her horse-to-be distracted her from thoughts of George. She couldn't wait to start checking out prospects. Maybe Max could give her some names to call that very afternoon. It was already Thursday, but Callie was sure she could set up some appointments for that weekend if she didn't waste any more time.

I wonder which would be better—a fairly young, green horse with lots of raw talent that I could bring along just the way I want, or an older, seasoned com-

petitor that can start entering races as soon as I've caught up? She chewed her lower lip, thinking about the pros and cons of both plans. Finally she decided to keep an open mind and see what came along. *And, of course, I should keep an open mind about breeds, too,* she reminded herself. *Just because I've always had good experiences with Arabians and Arab crosses doesn't mean they're all that's out there. Not that I'm going to seek out quarter horses or Shetland ponies, but it would be interesting to try out a few mustangs or Morgans or Appaloosas for a change. . . .*

She was so eager to get started that she could hardly sit still. Trying to distract herself, she tuned in to what the speaker, Ms. Norwood, was saying.

". . . and statistics show that more than half of all marriages will end in divorce," the woman was saying, her apple-cheeked face somber as she waggled one finger warningly at her audience. "There are plenty of reasons for that. Sometimes one spouse leaves a marriage to be with someone else. But even when there's no third party involved, there are a lot of factors that can come into play and drive emotions to the breaking point. Money issues. Disagreements about having and raising children. Lack of communication. Boredom. Growing apart. Jealousy. Even spouse abuse."

"I hear you, sister!" a loud voice came from near the back of the auditorium. "My wife is abusing me!"

Stevie had only been half paying attention as she

thought about her article, but she gasped when she recognized the voice that had spoken up. Spike!

This is the last straw, she thought furiously, spinning around in her seat. Sure enough, Spike was standing on his seat near the rear entrance, a big, self-satisfied grin on his face as students all over the auditorium craned their necks to see him.

Stevie leaped to her feet.

"Stevie, wait," Callie hissed, grabbing her arm. "Don't let him get to you."

Stevie shook off her friend's hand. *That's it,* she thought grimly. *He's embarrassed me for the last time!*

She jumped onto her seat and raised her fist in the air. *"I want a divorce!"* she screamed at the top of her lungs.

The auditorium erupted into pandemonium. After letting out her frustration and annoyance in one loud burst, Stevie immediately felt a lot better. She glanced around, a little surprised at the reaction her words had brought. A couple of rows away, Kenny Lamb and Moira Candell were arguing loudly and calling each other names. Across the aisle, Lorraine Olsen was complaining plaintively about how her partner cared more about surfing than he did about their relationship. Best of all, Veronica was standing up by her seat, yelling something about how Zach had only married her for her money and she wanted the marriage annulled due to geekiness.

Stevie grinned. *Cool*, she thought. *I guess Ms. Norwood was right when she said that stuff about driving emotions to the breaking point. It even works in fake marriages!*

A piercing whistle cut through the commotion. Miss Fenton was standing at the front of the stage, her thin face splotchy and red. "Silence!" she cried. "This is not a joke! I want you all to be silent, right now!"

"I can't be silent any longer!" a voice Stevie didn't recognize shouted from the other side of the room. "My wife won't listen to anything I say, and I won't take it anymore!"

"Me too," a girl's voice called out. "I would never marry a jerk like the one you matched me up with. He's the exact opposite of my type, anyway. This project is ridiculous."

Miss Fenton's face was turning redder and redder. She called for quiet a few more times, but it was hopeless. Students were shouting out complaints about their partners and the project from all directions. Ms. Norwood, still standing at the podium, gazed out at the students with undisguised horror.

Stevie was a little surprised that so many people seemed to be unhappy with their matches. But it also made sense when she thought about it. *It's not like a random computer pairing is the way to find true romance*, she thought. *I mean, I would never in a mil-*

lion years end up with a major dork like Spike. And there's no way someone like Veronica would get together with someone like Zach, either. Total mismatch.

She glanced over at Callie and Corey, who were watching in astonishment as more and more shouting matches erupted all over the auditorium. Even Alex, who was sitting on Stevie's other side, was arguing with Iris about all the money she was wasting on vitamin supplements and organic cat food.

Then again, maybe that's sort of the point, Stevie realized as she looked at Callie and Corey. They seemed like a great match in a lot of ways—they were both intelligent and likable and good-looking, and they seemed to get along great. As friends. But Stevie couldn't imagine them ever getting married for real. *People have to match up in a lot of ways. It's not enough for two people just to be nice, or smart, or good-looking. It's not even enough just being attracted to each other— though a lot of people I know seem to think that's the only really important thing. Maybe that's why so many couples that seem perfect together at first break up before long. I guess Phil and I are lucky that way. We got together because we had that instant attraction thing going for us. But we've stayed together because we're a good match in lots of other ways, too.*

She was distracted from her thoughts by the sight of Wesley Ward, Spike's soccer buddy, climbing up onto his seat in the front row and waving his arms. "Yo!" Wesley called, the neon green streak in his short, light brown hair gleaming beneath the auditorium lights. "Enough with the negativity, dudes!"

The noise level fell slightly as people stopped arguing long enough to see what was going on. Even Miss Fenton stopped shouting for a moment.

"What's he up to?" Stevie muttered curiously.

Callie shrugged, still looking a bit stunned at the outburst of anarchy. "Who knows?"

Wesley reached down and pulled his fake wife, Nicole Adams, up onto the seat beside him. She giggled and smoothed back her shoulder-length blond hair, glancing around the auditorium and waving to a friend or two. Stevie noticed that a few guys in the row behind Nicole were leaning forward in their seats, obviously hoping to get a peek up her short flouncy skirt.

Wesley held up his hand in a fist. "People!" he cried, slinging his free arm around Nicole's waist. "Didn't you ever hear the saying Make love, not war? We should all be trying to live up to our marriage vows, not break them!"

"Yeah!" Nicole said with another giggle. "All it takes is the right attitude."

Stevie rolled her eyes. "Yeah, right," she muttered to Callie. "Nicole's idea of the right attitude is going out with every guy who asks."

Wesley grinned down at Nicole. "My dear wife is right," he agreed loudly. "And to prove our point . . ." He wrapped his other arm around her and pulled her

191

closer, locking his lips on hers. Nicole didn't put up any protest. The two of them began making out enthusiastically as the entire auditorium erupted in whistles and cat calls.

"Mr. Ward! Miss Adams!" Miss Fenton screeched ineffectually. "Stop that this instant!"

But it was too late. Not only did Wesley and Nicole continue their very public display of affection, but several other couples immediately joined in the counterprotest.

Stevie felt a little sorry for the headmistress, who was waving her arms around like a windmill in a typhoon, but she also couldn't keep from laughing. "This is amazing!" she exclaimed, reaching for her notebook. "I've got to put this in my article. And I thought this project wasn't going to make exciting news!"

Callie and Corey chuckled, and Stevie glanced over at her brother with a grin to see if he'd heard. But Alex wasn't looking at her. He was staring intently toward the front of the room. Following his gaze, Stevie saw that he was watching Wesley and Nicole, who were still going at it with gusto.

Stevie frowned, suddenly remembering how Alex and Nicole had ended up together at that party when he and Lisa had briefly broken up. *I wonder . . .* , she thought with a stab of worry.

But she quickly pushed the thought aside. Flipping open her notebook, she began scribbling furiously. She didn't want to miss a single thing.

Stevie was still frantically making notes as she walked down the hall to her fourth-period class an hour later. She'd had to rethink the whole focus of her article to work in what had happened that morning. But she was excited about the new direction.

So this is what it's like, she thought, pausing in the middle of the crowded hallway as she tried to recall exactly what Wesley had said just before he and Nicole had started lip wrestling. She wanted to make sure she got the quote right. *I definitely see why people do this journalism stuff. You've always got to be on your toes or you might miss out on the story. And you've always got to be ready to change directions or you'll get left behind. It's exciting. It's unpredictable. I totally love it!*

She started walking again and immediately stepped squarely on a large, sneakered foot, realizing a split second too late that someone had stopped right in front of her. Glancing up to apologize, she saw that it was Scott. "Oh!" she said. "Hi. Sorry about that. You didn't need those toes, did you?"

Scott grinned. "Nope. I've got a spare set on the other foot," he joked. "So what's keeping you so distracted, as if I didn't know? I heard what happened in marriage class today."

Stevie nodded, glancing down at her notebook. "It was awesome," she said. "Theresa's going to love my article. As long as I can get it finished in time, that is. But it should be okay—I have a study hall fifth period, so I can get a lot of work done then."

"That's great," Scott said. "So are you still planning to go with the three-couples stuff, or—"

"Can we talk about it later?" Stevie broke in, shooting him a quick, apologetic smile. "I really want to—"

"No problem," Scott replied before she could finish. "I should have known better than to interrupt an intrepid journalist in the middle of a hot streak. So go, be creative and brilliant." He grinned. "Maybe I'll see you at Pine Hollow later and you can fill me in on the details."

"Okay. Thanks." Stevie smiled at him gratefully. It wasn't until he'd hurried away with a jaunty wave that she realized just what he'd said.

Is it just me, or has Scott been spending almost as much time at Pine Hollow lately as Callie has? she thought as she moved on toward her next class. *And it's not just showing up to drive her home or whatever. He's actually been hanging out, even though he almost never actually rides. Huh. That's kind of weird.*

But she didn't have time to think about it just then. She could worry about Scott's odd use of his free time later—*after* she finished her article.

THIRTEEN
13

Carole felt a twinge of guilt as she pulled her car to a stop in Pine Hollow's gravel parking area. *When Dad said I could go to the stable four times a week, he probably wasn't expecting me to head over here the first three days in a row,* she thought ruefully. Pulling her key from the ignition and opening the door, she shrugged and smiled. *Then again, maybe he did expect it. He knows me pretty well.*

Whatever her father thought of it, though, Carole hadn't been able to resist coming to the stable that day after school. She knew she would be busy that weekend—she was already committed to spending most of Saturday and Sunday working with Hometown Hope—so she wanted to get some quality time in at Pine Hollow while she could.

Pocketing her keys, she headed for the stable entrance, looking forward to a long session with Starlight.

When she entered the building, several excited-looking intermediate riders were standing in the entryway talking with Red O'Malley, Pine Hollow's head stable hand and Denise's longtime boyfriend. Red looked a bit harried, and for a moment Carole was tempted to go over and offer to give him a hand with whatever crisis was brewing. But after a glance at her watch, she decided she didn't have time. Her father was due home from his trip by three o'clock or so, which meant that Carole was going to have to walk in the door herself by five on the dot, or she could kiss their new arrangement good-bye. And she couldn't stand that. The very thought of being banned from the stable again made her queasy.

Giving Red a quick, only slightly guilty wave, Carole hurried past, heading straight for the tack room. She glanced into the office as she left a moment later with Starlight's saddle and bridle, but it was empty.

Soon she was buckling the throatlatch on her horse's bridle. "There we are," she told the horse as she tightened his noseband. "Almost ready to go. So what do you feel like doing today, boy? Want to practice our flatwork? Or maybe do a little jumping?"

Starlight snorted, which Carole interpreted to mean *Whatever you want to do is fine with me.* She smiled and rubbed the horse under his jaws before leading him down the aisle. It had been so long since she'd really been focused on the ongoing process of training her horse that she wasn't sure where to start.

She decided to solve that problem by doing a little of everything.

"That way we'll figure out what we need to work on," she murmured as she led the big bay gelding out to the little-used west paddock, where they weren't likely to be disturbed. "Plus it'll be fun."

She was right about that. For the next hour, she put everything out of her mind except her horse. They practiced their reverses, they worked on extension and collection for a while, they even did a little jumping over some low cross rails. It felt wonderful to spend that much time in the saddle thinking about nothing but her horse. *This is what I've been missing so much,* she thought as Starlight sailed easily over the jump, tossing his head on landing as if expressing how much he, too, was enjoying himself. *This is why I can never let myself get banned from the stable again.* She knew that one of the surest ways to avoid that was never to miss her two-hour curfew.

All too soon, it was time to head inside. As she reluctantly pulled up and started walking her horse around the paddock to cool him down, she realized that it had been a long time since she'd been able to enjoy a nice long session like the one she'd just had with Starlight without having to worry about squeezing her own riding in between doing chores, teaching riding lessons, waiting for the grain delivery, and the million and one other things she had to worry about as a member of Pine Hollow's small staff.

It's kind of nice to be able to relax and not think about that kind of stuff, now that I'm not working here anymore, she thought as she led Starlight toward the paddock gate. *Maybe that should be telling me something about which career is right for me. Do I really want to do something where I'm going to end up caring for lots of horses like Max does as a riding instructor and stable manager? Or would I be better off riding and training one or just a few horses, like I would if I decided to become a competitive rider?*

She frowned, thinking about that. There were positive and negative aspects about both options.

Then again, maybe I could find a job that sort of combines the best parts of both worlds, she thought. *Like becoming a full-time professional trainer . . .*

It wasn't until she felt Starlight nudge her sharply on the shoulder that she realized her steps had slowed almost to a stop as she pondered her choices. "Oops!" she said, patting the horse before moving on more briskly toward the stable entrance. "Sorry about that, boy. I know you're eager to get inside and have a nice long drink and a snack. And you definitely deserve it." Putting thoughts of the future on hold for the moment, she hurried inside to take care of her horse.

A short while later Starlight was resting comfortably in his stall, freshly groomed with clean straw underfoot, a full bucket of clean, clear water hanging on the back wall, and a rack of fragrant hay in the corner. "Okay, boy," Carole said, giving the horse a pat on the rump as she took a last look around the stall. "I think you're all set." She glanced at her watch. "Just in time, too. I've got to be in the door in twenty minutes."

That left her plenty of time to get home, since it was only a ten-minute drive from the stable to her house. But she figured it wouldn't hurt to show up a little early—just to show her father that she was taking the new rules seriously.

She let herself out of Starlight's stall and headed toward the exit, humming softly under her breath. As sorry as she was to have to leave—it would have been nice to be able to hang out, maybe help with the evening chores or see if any of her friends were around or just visit with some of the other horses— it was a little easier to drag herself away when she knew she could come back again the next day. After that, she would have to manage for a couple of days away, but even that wouldn't be too bad. And there were only a few weeks left before New Year's, when she hoped her father would lift the restrictions altogether.

She had just reached the front doors when she heard someone calling her name. Turning, she saw Red O'Malley rushing toward her across the stable entryway, an anxious expression on his freckled face.

"Hi, Red," she said. "Is anything wrong?"

"Just *everything*!" Red exclaimed, throwing up his hands. "Denise is home sick, and Max had to leave a little while ago to pick up Deborah—her car broke down somewhere up toward Maryland." He glanced over his shoulder frantically. "I'm supposed to be helping the adult trail class tack up right now—they scheduled this moonlight ride and wine-and-cheese-picnic thing ages ago, so I absolutely can't cancel—but I also need to keep an eye on the beginners who just finished out in the schooling ring, plus do about fourteen other things. I even enlisted Callie's brother to help out by manning the phones for a while—and he doesn't even ride here!"

"Where's, um, Ben?" Carole asked, trying not to reveal any unnecessary emotion at the mention of that particular name. "Can't he help you out with the adult class or the beginners?"

"He's not back yet," Red replied. At Carole's confused look, he explained, "He asked Max if he could take an hour off this afternoon, and he's not due back for ten minutes or so—he swore he'd be here in plenty of time to teach the Adams girl's private lesson at five, since Denise isn't here to do it." He clutched at his carrot-colored hair and stared at Carole beseechingly. "So how about it? I know you're not an official employee anymore, but can you help me out? Just until Ben gets back?"

Carole hesitated, peeking at her watch. She had to leave in the next ten minutes if she wanted to make it home in time. *But that's probably longer than I'll need,* she thought. *Ben never stays away from this place for long if he can help it. He'll probably be back early—as in any second now.*

"Okay," she told Red. "What do you want me to do?"

Red sent her off to supervise the beginning riders as they untacked and groomed their horses. That went smoothly enough, though Carole couldn't help feeling more and more anxious as minute after minute ticked by with no sign of Ben. *Where could he be?* Carole wondered, checking her watch for the umpteenth time. *It's not like him to be late. But if he doesn't get back soon, he will be. And so will I.*

Soon her ten minutes had come and gone. Carole tried to tell herself that her father wouldn't notice if she was five minutes late. Five minutes later, she almost managed to convince herself that ten minutes one way or the other wasn't a big deal. But when fifteen minutes had passed and Ben still hadn't returned, she was starting to feel frantic. Red had already left with the adult trail group, and aside from Scott, Carole was the only person at the stable over the age of nine.

It didn't help when Nicole Adams arrived a few minutes after five, impatient to get started. "Where's Denise?" she demanded immediately, tossing her wavy blond hair restlessly when she found Carole in the student locker room.

"She's out sick today," Carole said, pulling her attention away from the seven-year-old rider whose tight boots she was trying to yank off. "Ben Marlow's going to be teaching your lesson instead."

"Really!" Nicole pursed her lips, looking interested. "He's kind of cute. So where is he?"

Carole almost laughed as she pictured Nicole trying to flirt with Ben, who seemed quite immune to her sort of obvious charms. But that image aside, she wasn't feeling very amused at the moment. What was her father going to say when she finally made it home? How picky was he going to be about that two-hour limit?

Dad knows that you can't always time things exactly when it comes to horses, Carole thought uncertainly. *He's not going to condemn me for a lousy fifteen minutes, is he? I could tell him that Starlight threw a shoe, or that I had to wait for someone to help me bring down more hay. . . .*

She sighed. Maybe that was true. Maybe her father would let fifteen minutes slide. But unless she left the stable at that very moment, she was going to be even later than that. And there was a limit to any parent's understanding.

"Ben will be here soon," she told Nicole, trying not to let her anxiety show. "Why don't you go tack up Diablo? That way you'll be ready when he turns up."

Nicole nodded and hurried off, and soon Carole

had dispatched the beginning rider, too, minus her too-small boots. She sat back on the bench and stared at her watch, wishing she could slow down its steady, inexorable ticking.

If I leave right now and break the speed limit the whole way, I could probably get home before Dad's head explodes, she thought. *There might still be time to explain things to him, to make him understand that this wasn't my fault.*

She chewed on her lip for a second, tempted. All she had to do was run over to the office and tell Scott he was on his own. He could handle things for a few minutes until Ben got back, or until Callie came in from the trails and could help out. Nobody would care if the phone didn't get answered for a little while. And it would be a piece of cake for him to charm Nicole into being patient about her delayed lesson. . . .

But almost before she completed the thought, Carole sank back in her seat again and sighed, knowing she couldn't do it. Scott might be able to handle Nicole, but there was no way he could deal with eight or ten cranky, overtired, and potentially careless beginning riders at the same time. He wasn't a rider—he couldn't be expected to remind the little kids not to walk around near their horses' hind legs or help them untangle knotted reins or explain the difference between straw and hay.

And what if Ben doesn't get back soon? she added

hopelessly. *Red's trail ride won't be finished for quite a while, and Nicole definitely isn't going to want to wait around for him. Plus, Max would be really angry if he found out the stable was left unattended. He'd probably be kind of mad at me, but he left Red in charge, so he'd really come down on him. Not to mention how angry he'd be with Ben for breaking his word to be back by five. I'm sure he never would've left in the first place if he'd known Ben was going to be so late.*

She gulped, knowing what she had to do. Standing up before she could think too hard about what the consequences might be, she headed for the door to check on the beginners' progress.

Ten minutes later Carole was in the tack room overseeing the last of the beginners' cleaning chores when Nicole appeared in the doorway. "There you are," she said, looking mildly put out. "Where's Ben? Diablo's all tacked up. I'm ready to start my lesson."

Carole gulped, hiding her dismay by turning to shoo the beginning rider out of the room. "Um, did you ask Scott?"

"Uh-huh. He said he hasn't seen him."

Carole checked the time. Ben was really late. Could he possibly have forgotten that he was supposed to come back to the stable after he finished whatever he was doing? It didn't seem likely. But then, it didn't seem likely that he would be as late as he already was, either.

I could just go ahead and teach Nicole's lesson myself,

she thought. *Of course, that would mean I'd be so totally and incredibly late that there's no way Dad would ever trust me again.*

"Um . . ." Carole glanced helplessly at Nicole, wondering what to do. She was trying to come up with the right words to ask her to be patient for just a few more minutes to see if Ben turned up. But before she could open her mouth again, she heard rapid footsteps coming down the hall toward the tack room.

Ben? she thought hopefully, feeling her heart lift slightly. Maybe there was still time—maybe she could still race home and beg her father for forgiveness.

But her hopes were dashed a moment later when Veronica diAngelo appeared in the doorway behind Nicole. "Hey, Nic," she said irritably. "It's like twenty-five after. I thought you said your lesson started at five."

"It was supposed to," Nicole replied with a shrug. "Only trouble is, they seem to be fresh out of teachers at this place."

Veronica glanced at Carole briefly but didn't bother to do anything else to acknowledge her presence. "Well, if you don't get started soon, we're going to be late for the movie," she said. "And the guys are meeting us there—I don't have any way to reach them. Neither one of them has a cell phone, or even a beeper." She rolled her heavily lined eyes heavenward as if such an idea were almost unthinkable.

Nicole looked perturbed. "I don't want to miss the movie," she said, casting an anxious glance at Carole. "Maybe I should just give this lesson a pass."

"Maybe you should," Veronica agreed coolly. "And then maybe you should sign up for lessons someplace where they're a little more organized."

Carole gasped. She couldn't believe Veronica would say such a thing. After all, she'd taken lessons at Pine Hollow herself for years. Of course, she'd tangled with Max and Red and just about everyone else on the staff during the course of those years, too. Maybe it shouldn't have been such a surprise that she was so quick to try to sabotage Max's business.

Besides, she reminded herself with a nervous gulp, *Veronica knows how important Pine Hollow is to Stevie. And didn't Stevie say just yesterday that Veronica keeps threatening her with horrible revenge because of that article?*

Carole knew that Veronica's opinion carried a lot of weight with her cliquey friends. If Nicole didn't have her lesson that day, Veronica would probably make a huge deal of it, just to spite Stevie. Carole certainly didn't want to be the reason that Max lost a paying customer. Especially since, technically, it would be Ben's fault, and that would mean he would be in even more trouble for being late.

"Don't worry, Nicole," she said quickly. "Um, since Ben doesn't seem to be back yet—"

"Ben?" Veronica interrupted, wrinkling her nose.

"You mean that dark-haired guy with the bad attitude? No wonder you're having trouble, Nic. If I were you, I'd complain good and loud about being stuck with him."

Carole felt her face turn red, but she kept her gaze focused on Nicole. "Um, as I was saying, maybe I'll just teach your lesson instead. We can start right now. Okay?"

Nicole looked slightly disappointed, but she nodded. "Sure," she agreed. "But let's hurry up and get going, okay? I've wasted enough time." She glanced at Veronica. "Sorry you have to wait around for me."

"That's okay," Veronica told her. "I figured I'd hang out and watch your lesson, as long as you don't mind." As Nicole nodded agreeably, Veronica turned to Carole. "By the way," she said casually, "is that obnoxious friend of yours around?"

"Let me take a wild guess," Carole said. "Are you by any chance referring to Stevie?"

Veronica nodded. "I was hoping to talk to her about, uh, some homework."

Yeah, right, Carole thought. She was sure that Veronica was there to find out if Stevie had backed down from including her and Zach in her article. *Fat chance of that*, Carole added silently. *If I know Stevie—and I think I do—the fact that Veronica is so worked up about this probably made her even more eager to stick with her original plan.*

She didn't bother explaining that to Veronica, though. "No," she said instead, pasting an innocent expression on her face. "I think she's been busy all afternoon finishing up that little article she's writing for your school paper."

Veronica scowled, and Carole hid a smile by glancing down at her watch. As she did, she suddenly felt a lot less like smiling. Five-thirty. She could almost feel her riding privileges slipping away . . . maybe for a lot longer than the few weeks until New Year's. But what choice did she have?

"Ready?" she said to Nicole. "Come on, let's work in the indoor ring."

As she approached the turnoff for Pine Hollow, Stevie checked the clock on the dashboard of her car. It read 6:47, which meant that it was actually about a quarter to six. *I've got to remember to reset that thing for daylight savings time,* she thought absently, hitting her blinker for the turn. Her parents wouldn't expect her for dinner until six-thirty, which left her plenty of time to stop in at the stable and share her great news with anyone who happened to be around.

Soon she was hurrying through the early-evening darkness toward the brightly lit stable. Pulling open the door and stepping inside, she shivered slightly as she shook off the December chill.

I still can't believe Theresa was so excited about my article! she thought gleefully as she paused near the door to strip off her driving gloves. *I mean, I believe it, because I know it's true, and I knew it would happen. But I still can't believe it!*

She'd just come from her meeting with the editor in chief. Theresa wouldn't make any promises, but she'd assured Stevie that she would show her article to the other editors and see if they could work it into the next day's issue. That was all Stevie needed to hear.

They'll find space for it, she thought confidently. *And then I can just sit back and bask in the glow of my new career as a star reporter!*

She couldn't wait to share her news with someone. She'd noticed that Scott's car was parked in the lot outside, along with Carole's dark red junker. That meant both of them were at the stable somewhere, along with Callie.

I'm glad Scott likes to hang around this place so much, she thought with a smile. *Because even if Callie's still out on the trail testing her night vision and Carole's busy at the manure pit or somewhere, there will at least be one person here to listen to my tale of triumph!*

Hearing the faint sound of hoofbeats from the indoor ring, Stevie walked over and peeked through the wooden doors, which were partially ajar. The first person she spotted was Carole, who was on foot in the middle of the ring, watching as Diablo cantered around her in a tight circle.

Then Stevie recognized Diablo's rider. She

209

frowned. "Nicole?" she muttered. At the sight of the other girl, Stevie couldn't stop her usual suspicions from popping into her head.

I know she used to ride here, and I know Max claims she was pretty good as a little kid, Stevie thought, staring at Nicole as she skillfully steered her horse through a smooth reverse. *But she gave that up years ago. She lost interest. And suddenly she decides to start riding again? I don't buy it. I still think she's hanging out here hoping to spend time with Alex. Why else would someone with no apparent interest in horses decide to start spending so much time at the stable?*

"Hi, Stevie," Scott called, appearing at the mouth of the hallway leading to the stable office. "What are you doing here?"

Stevie froze. Suddenly the truth hit her with the force of an eighteen-wheeler. *Nicole isn't the only one who's been spending her free time here lately,* she thought with a gulp. *Wasn't I just thinking how weird it is that Scott is here so much when he doesn't even ride? Well, maybe there's a reason for that. Maybe he's hanging out here because he's interested in someone who rides here. Someone like . . . me!*

It was a crazy thought, but it also made perfect sense. Stevie and Scott had spent a lot of time together a month or so before when she'd run his campaign for student body president. What if he'd come away from that with the wrong idea about their relationship? What if he had a crush on her?

"Stevie? Are you okay?"

With a start, she realized that she hadn't returned Scott's greeting. Instead, she was staring at him with her eyes wide in horror and shock. "Ulp," she said. "Um, I mean, hi. Everything's fine, just fine."

Scott wrinkled his brow and cocked his head to one side, studying her carefully. "Are you sure?" he asked, taking a couple of steps toward her.

"Yep! Totally sure!" Stevie yelped, hopping backward so fast that she crashed into the ring door. "Ow!"

"Are you okay?" Scott looked more concerned than ever. He hurried toward her, putting one hand on her arm.

Stevie yanked her arm away, pretending she just wanted to lean over and rub her leg where it had hit the door. "Oh, sure," she said hastily. "I'm just a klutz, that's all. Phil is always teasing me about it. You know—my boyfriend, Phil?"

Scott looked puzzled now. "Sure, I know Phil," he said. "But are you sure you're okay? You hit that door pretty hard."

Stevie nodded vigorously, standing up straight and dodging away until she'd put a good five feet between them. "I'm fine," she assured him. Darting closer just long enough to give him a friendly punch on the arm, she added, "but thanks for asking, buddy."

Scott winced and rubbed his arm where she'd punched him. "If I didn't know better, I'd think you'd just hit your head instead of your leg," he commented. "What's going on, Stevie?" Suddenly he blinked, and his look of confusion shifted to one of concern. "Hey, wait a minute. You just had your meeting with Theresa, right? Are you upset because of that? Didn't she like your story?"

"Oh! No, actually she thought it was great." Stevie smiled, flashing back once again to Theresa's compliments. Then, remembering how Phil always said that her smile was one of her cutest qualities, Stevie pursed her lips together tightly in a straight line. "It sounds like she's probably going to run it in tomorrow's *Sentinel*. Thanks for asking."

"That's great." Scott frowned. "But listen, if you don't mind my asking, are you nervous about something? And why are you making that face?"

"This face?" Stevie relaxed her mouth slightly. "Um, no reason. Actually, Phil loves it when I make this face." She let out a short, nervous laugh, realizing that she was babbling but somehow unable to stop herself. "But then again, I guess that's how it is when you're in love. Which we are. Very much in love. Me and Phil."

Scott was backing away slightly. "Look, I know you're psyched about this article," he said uncertainly, "but I really hope you didn't decide to do anything stupid, like celebrate with a few beers or something."

"Nope." Stevie gulped, realizing it was definitely

time to tone it down. "But thanks for your concern. You're a great friend. Almost like another brother. Not that I need any more." She let out a slightly hysterical giggle as the stable door opened and Lisa came inside, shaking off the cold.

Scott gave her one last doubtful glance. "Um, whatever," he said. "If you're sure you're okay, I think I'll go say hi to Lisa."

Stevie sighed with relief as he headed across the entryway to intercept her friend. *No wonder he was so eager to make his escape,* she thought wryly. *I guess I was starting to sound kind of insane there. That should do the trick. Who wants to date a total wacko?*

Before she could decide whether to be relieved or embarrassed, she spotted Veronica emerging from the office hallway. "Stevie Lake!" Veronica snapped instantly. "I want to talk to you."

Yikes. What's she doing here? Stevie wondered. "Um, sorry. I was just on my way out," she said. She shot a quick glance into the ring, where Carole still seemed to be oblivious to her presence. Then she looked over at Lisa, who was laughing at something Scott was saying. As much as Stevie wanted to share her news with her two best friends, she wanted to avoid Veronica even more. She was too rattled by her new theory about Scott to deal with the other girl's ill-tempered whining at the moment. Besides, if Stevie could just manage to avoid her until the next morning, the article would be printed for all to read and it would be too late for Veronica to protest any further.

Veronica was barreling toward her, her dark eyes shooting fire, but Stevie was just a few feet from the entrance to the stable aisle. Sprinting for it, she took the turn and hurried toward Belle's stall. Realizing that was the first place Veronica would look, she ducked instead into Windsor's stall across the aisle. Giving the big, calm gelding a quick pat, she crouched down and pasted herself against the wall, out of sight of anyone passing by. A moment later she heard rapid footsteps hurrying past.

"Stevie?" Veronica sounded peeved. "Give it up, I know you're in—"

She cut herself off in midsentence. Stevie covered her mouth with her hand to stop herself from laughing. Even though she couldn't see Veronica, she could picture her vexed expression perfectly. She was probably leaning over the half door of Belle's stall, scanning every inch of the place to see if Stevie might actually be hiding under the straw bedding or behind the water bucket.

A moment later, she heard footsteps moving off more slowly down the aisle. Stevie gave Veronica a few minutes to round the corner at the end of the U-shaped aisle, then let herself out of Windsor's stall and hurried to let herself into Belle's.

"Don't give me away, okay, girl?" she whispered as

the horse wandered over to greet her. She reached up to rub Belle's smooth coppery neck. "I just need to hide out in here for a few minutes until she gives up and goes away." She gulped, thinking of Scott. "Until *everyone* gives up and goes away."

FOURTEEN

Lisa's stomach was tying itself into knots as she walked slowly toward Eve's stall. Alex would be arriving any minute now for their predinner trail ride, and she wasn't sure she was ready. She'd spent the past twenty-four hours thinking about it, and she knew what she had to do, but that didn't mean it was going to be easy.

"Hey, lady," she greeted Eve softly as the gentle gray mare came forward to meet her. "Feel like a nice ride?" She slipped off her heavy down jacket—it was warm in the stable—and hung it over the half door of the stall. Then she set to work getting the mare ready.

To distract herself from worrying about the coming ride, she thought about Stevie. *Scott said she was acting really weird,* she thought. *And it is kind of strange that she ran off like that without even saying hello to me. I guess it's like I said—she was just so happy about her article getting accepted that she went a little crazy. That sure sounds like Stevie to me.*

She smiled and shook her head as she gave Eve's silvery body a quick brushing. She'd long since learned not to try too hard to figure out Stevie's reactions to stuff.

The important part is that things are going well for her, she told herself. *She's been so excited about this newspaper deal, and now it sounds like she's off to a great start. And then there's Carole—her life seems to be on an upswing now, too. And it's about time.*

It was really nice to see Carole back at Pine Hollow again. Lisa had noticed her friend in the indoor ring as she walked past, though Carole hadn't seen her.

But after a few minutes, even thoughts of her friends' good fortunes couldn't keep her mind off the coming ride. When Eve was ready, Lisa left her cross-tied in the aisle and started pacing, walking to the end of the U and back again, taking long, deep, cleansing breaths with each step. Just when she wasn't sure she could stand it any longer, she heard footsteps heading her way. Spinning around, she saw Alex hurrying toward her.

"Hi!" he said, taking her hand and pulling her toward him for a quick hello kiss. "Scott said you were over here. Are you ready to go? I just finished tacking up Congo."

Lisa nodded mutely. To hide her consternation, she turned and fussed with Eve's tack as Alex hurried off to get his horse. *It's going to be okay,* she told herself as she led Eve down the aisle. *No matter what happens, everything's going to be fine.*

They led their horses outside and mounted. The last traces of sun had already vanished from the evening sky, but a nearly full moon was rising, giving a bright, silvery glow to the pastures and field surrounding Pine Hollow.

"It's too late to head into the woods," Lisa said, doing her best to sound normal. She wanted to wait for just the right moment to say what she had to say. "Why don't we just ride over to the cow field?"

Alex nodded agreeably, and they set off. The trail to the cow field was an underappreciated route among Pine Hollow's younger riders, though Lisa thought it was the perfect choice for an evening ride. It led halfway down the stable's driveway, through the front pasture, past a stand of small ornamental trees in front of Max's house, and along the road for a few hundred yards, before finally bringing riders to the edge of a large, gently rolling meadow dotted with trees. During the summer, a local farmer grazed a few dairy cows on the lush grass, but in the colder months the cows went elsewhere, though Lisa had no idea where.

She didn't feel much like talking as they set off on the familiar trail. Alex chattered a bit about his sister's journalistic triumph, and Lisa did her best to respond intelligibly. She was relieved when they reached the narrow path along the road, which required them to ride single file. *Do I really want to do this?* she wondered anxiously, staring ahead at Alex's back as he swayed along with Congo's steady stride. *Is it the right thing for us—for me?*

There was no way to know for sure. Lisa didn't like that feeling of uncertainty, but it didn't change what she had to do.

Finally they reached the cow field. Alex leaned over to release the latch on the gate, and Lisa urged Eve through it. They rode a little farther into the field, cresting a slight rise, which gave them a view of the whole place.

A thin veil of mist was creeping up from the network of streams that ran through the area, giving the meadow an eerie look in the moonlight. "This is beautiful," Lisa said in a hushed tone, forgetting about her problems for a moment as she took in the sight of the gnarled branches of an ancient maple tree stretching toward the low-hanging moon.

"Yeah," Alex agreed, riding up beside her. "Want to stop for a few and check it out?" He gestured toward a large fallen tree trunk that rested against the hillside just below, forming a natural bench.

Lisa nodded. Swinging her right leg over Eve's hindquarters, she jumped down lightly from the mare's saddle and led her horse to a small tree nearby. She'd brought a halter along, which she quickly slipped on over the mare's bridle. Soon Eve was safely tied to the tree, her girth loosened and her big teeth already at work on the grass.

Alex didn't bother to tie up Congo, instead leaving the calm, well-trained gelding ground-tied beside Eve. Then he walked over and put both arms around Lisa's waist. "Well," he said, his voice husky. "Here we are. Alone at last."

Lisa drew back slightly, feeling nervous. The moment was here. Could she do it?

"Yeah," she said. "Um, and I'm glad. Because—"

"Me too." Alex didn't give her a chance to finish her sentence. Instead, he pulled her close, wrapping his arms around her so tightly that she could hardly breathe. Bending down, he covered her mouth with his own.

For a moment Lisa felt herself being swept away in his kiss. But she resisted the feeling and pushed him away. "Wait," she said breathlessly. "That's not what I meant."

"Oh really? Then how about this." This time Alex sank onto the fallen log, pulling her down onto his lap before she could resist. He buried one hand in her blond hair and his other hand rested on her thigh as he kissed her again. Lisa's heart was pounding so loudly that it seemed to echo in her head.

I don't have to say anything, she told herself, feeling her resolve weaken as Alex's kisses traveled from her lips down her chin to her throat. *Being here with him feels so good, so familiar . . . I could just relax and go along with this feeling and forget about everything else. . . .*

But as tempting as that was, she knew she couldn't do it. Wimping out now wouldn't change anything. Tomorrow she would just have to deal with the same problems again, the same mixed-up feelings.

"Stop," she gasped, shoving Alex away sharply.

He blinked. "Huh?" he said. "What? Is something wrong?"

"We have to talk."

"Now?" Alex tugged at the neck of her jacket, pulling her toward him again. "Are you sure there isn't something else you'd rather do?"

"No." This time Lisa stood up, moving several steps away and then turning to face him with her arms crossed over her chest. "This can't wait, Alex. It's—It's about us."

"What about us?" Alex looked nervous. He sat up straighter on the log, running a hand through his slightly rumpled brown hair.

Lisa took a deep breath. "I—I'm not sure how to say it," she said, looking straight into his eyes. "I just think you need to know—I haven't been feeling right lately. About us, I mean."

"What are you saying?" Alex asked cautiously.

"I'm not exactly sure." Lisa shrugged helplessly. "It's just that things don't feel the same anymore."

"Oh." Alex looked uncertain. "Um, I guess I know

what you mean, sort of. But so what? Things change, the world doesn't stop for anyone. All we can do is deal with it, right?"

"I guess." Lisa bit her lip. "It's just that I'm afraid that after, you know, everything that's happened lately . . ." She paused for a moment, not wanting to dredge it all up again. The arguments. The jealousy. The long separations. "Well, I'm just thinking that maybe we've sort of grown apart."

"What?" Alex looked startled. "What do you mean?"

Lisa felt strange, as though she were somehow merely a spectator to this whole conversation. It couldn't actually be happening, could it? But somehow it was, the words pouring out as if she were sitting in an audience watching it all play out onstage. As if it were happening to someone else. "I mean I'm not sure we're connecting the way we used to," she said quietly. "I'm not—I'm just not sure things are working out the way they are now. Not anymore."

"Oh." Alex looked down at his hands, which were dangling between his knees as he perched on the log. His face was hidden in shadow, and Lisa leaned forward, wanting to know how he was feeling.

"It's not that I've stopped loving you," she said, tears springing to her eyes so quickly that it caught her by surprise. Suddenly it didn't feel like this was happening to someone else anymore. It was happening to her—to her and Alex. How could that be?

How could they have come to this? "It's not that. It's just that—that something has to change. I'm not sure exactly what it is, but . . ." She gulped, unable to continue as she struggled to maintain control of her emotions.

"I know." Alex looked up at her again, and the moonlight revealed sadness on his face—but not surprise. "I should have said something sooner, but I was being a wimp. I've noticed it, too."

"R-Really?" Sinking down onto the log beside him, Lisa wiped at a tear that had escaped and was trickling down her cheek.

"Yeah."

They were both silent for a moment. Finally Lisa cleared her throat. "Um, so what do you think we should do?"

Alex absently ran one hand through his hair. "I don't know. That's the problem. I knew something was, like, *off* with us. I just wasn't sure what it was or how to fix it." He gave her a wan, sheepish smile. "I guess that's why I was pawing at you like that just now. I was sort of hoping . . . well, it sounds stupid now. But I was thinking maybe that was all we needed to get back to where we were. Back when all we could think about was being close to each other."

Lisa wasn't sure what to say. How could they both have been having these feelings without either of them realizing that the other was feeling the same way?

"I thought everything would be perfect again after

223

my grounding ended." Alex sighed. "But it isn't. Something's still missing, like you said."

Lisa picked at the hem of her jacket. She couldn't help feeling a little hurt at Alex's words. Why wasn't she enough for him anymore? What was missing? "So what should we do now?" she asked again, glancing up to meet his eye only when she was sure she wasn't going to start bawling uncontrollably.

Alex stared at her, his familiar hazel eyes shadowy and dark in the moonlight. "I don't know."

Lisa realized that she'd been hoping, up until this very point, that this would do it. That she and Alex would talk things out and somehow, magically, everything would be better. But it wasn't working out that way. True, she felt relieved to have the problem out in the open. But that hadn't made it go away. "We can't just go on like this and wait for something to change," she said, thinking aloud.

"Can't we?" Alex's hand strayed to her knee and he stroked it softly, so softly that she could barely feel his touch through her jeans. "Don't people do that all the time? And it's not like things are so terrible between us right now. . . ."

Lisa shook her head. "That won't work," she said softly. "If we want things to change, we have to do something to change them."

"Okay," Alex agreed with a slight frown. He cleared his throat. "Then maybe we need to try something—something more radical."

"Like what?" Lisa asked quickly, knowing the answer but not wanting to be the one to say it.

Alex stared at her, his eyes sad. "Like maybe we need to take a break for a while. From each other."

Even though she'd known the words were coming—even though she'd been thinking them herself—they still hit Lisa like a punch to the gut. The tears returned, and this time more of them spilled over before she could stop them. Still, she wasn't going to back down now. "I—I think you're right," she managed to choke out. "I think that's a good idea."

On one level, it didn't seem possible. How could they even be thinking of doing this? Hadn't they spent most of the past few months bemoaning the fact that they didn't have enough time together? And now that they were finally free to be together all the time, were they actually planning to break up?

No, not break up, Lisa told herself firmly as she wiped her eyes on her coat sleeve. *Just take a break. There's a difference.*

When she looked at Alex, she saw that his eyes were moist, too. "Um, so how should we . . . ," he said helplessly.

For a second, as they stared at each other in the eerie, silvery light of the moonlit meadow, Lisa was tempted to take it all back. *I was just being silly,* she could say. *You're right—things aren't that bad. We love each other, and that's enough. . . .*

But it wasn't. Not really. There was no going back

now, no matter how tempting it was to just forget her worries, kiss him like there was no tomorrow, and hope that all the problems would just go away by themselves. The world didn't work that way, and Lisa knew it.

She cleared her throat again. "Let's give it until New Year's," she said firmly. "We'll talk again then and see how we feel. Then we can, you know, take it from there."

Alex nodded. "Okay," he said in a small voice. "New Year's."

"Oh!" Suddenly Lisa thought of something else. "And I think we have to both agree to—to see other people."

Alex looked startled, but he nodded again. "Agreed." He gulped. "Even though it will be really weird."

"I know." Lisa couldn't quite imagine what it would be like to date another guy now, after being with Alex for so long, but she knew that the only way this experiment would work was if they really thought about their options. And they couldn't do that if they both spent the next month moping around alone, counting the days until New Year's.

Besides, maybe dating other people will do the trick, she thought hopefully. *It could be just the thing to make us appreciate what we really have with each other.*

There was a long moment of silence, each of them thinking. Finally, though, Alex clapped his hands on his knees and stood. "Okay, now that that's settled, maybe we should head back."

Lisa nodded, realizing with a shiver that she was getting cold sitting there. "Good idea." She stood up beside him, intending to head straight over to the horses, who were still grazing nearby.

But Alex stopped her with a touch on the shoulder. "Wait," he said softly.

Lisa stopped and turned, tilting her head back to look at him. For a few endless seconds, they just gazed into each other's eyes. Then Alex lifted his hands to her face and pulled her gently toward him. Their lips met briefly, barely brushing each other before the kiss was over. Lisa wasn't even sure which of them pulled back first.

They didn't say a word as they walked over to the horses, side by side, and prepared to mount. And they remained silent throughout the ride back to Pine Hollow. Lisa wasn't surprised. They'd said all there was to say.

Carole was feeling frantic as she hurried down the hall to the stable office forty minutes later. Nicole's lesson had finally ended a few minutes earlier, leaving Carole with the realization that she still couldn't go. Red wasn't back from the trail ride yet, and Ben hadn't returned from wherever he was, either. Worse yet, Scott seemed to have disappeared, too.

She had tried to call her father right after Nicole's

lesson but had gotten the machine. She'd almost hung up, hoping that her father had been delayed somehow. Maybe he didn't even know she was late!

But she resisted the temptation. At the sound of the beep, she'd left a brief message, telling him that she was still at the stable and not to worry.

I can't just leave the stable unattended, Carole had thought desperately as she'd hung up the phone and headed down the hall to see if Nicole needed any help with her horse. She and Veronica were in a hurry, and Carole suspected that if she didn't step in, Diablo wouldn't get much of a grooming that evening. *I don't have a key to the alarm system anymore, and besides, someone has to make evening rounds. Anyway, it's not like a few more minutes are going to make much difference at this point. I'm already toast.*

She tried not to think about that as she flipped through the stable's journal, checking to see if any of the horses needed special medications or treatments that evening. She didn't see anything that required immediate attention, so she left the office and wandered back down the hall, trying to figure out what to do next to keep herself busy until Red returned. She'd just about given up on Ben at that point.

I wish I'd been able to catch Stevie or Lisa, she thought, pausing in the entryway and glancing around uncertainly. *They definitely would have pitched in to help me out if they knew what was up, and I'm pretty sure they were here earlier, since Belle and Eve were both freshly groomed when I checked on them just now. But I guess they're gone.*

Realizing that there was one way to check on that, she walked quickly to the front doors and swung them open, peering out into the darkness. It was already pretty cold outside, and a brisk night wind was adding to the chill. Wrapping her arms around herself, Carole took a couple of steps outside until she could see past the fence of the schooling ring. A single spotlight illuminated the parking lot across the driveway, and Carole immediately saw that the only car still parked there was her own.

With a resigned sigh, she stepped back into the relative warmth of the entryway. She was about to pull the doors shut again and head over to the stable aisle to check on the horses when she caught the flash of headlights swinging into the end of the drive.

Her heart jumped hopefully. Was it Ben? Or maybe Stevie or Lisa had forgotten something and returned. Or Scott and Callie had come back, realizing that she still needed help. . . .

But when the car pulled into the parking area, its tires shooting gravel as it took the turn a little too quickly, Carole gulped. "Dad," she whispered, feeling her heart sink like a stone.

She quickly stepped back into the entryway, her heart pounding. *Maybe I can still explain,* she thought, biting her lip nervously. *Maybe he'll understand if I tell him exactly what happened.*

But when her father entered a moment later, he didn't even give her a chance to open her mouth. "There you are!" he exclaimed, his face pinched with anger. "I couldn't believe it when I got your message. I had to see it with my own two eyes. But yes, here you are, standing right here in the stable as if you didn't have a curfew at all. Young lady, I don't think I've ever been as angry with you as I am right now!"

"But Dad!" Carole protested desperately. "Please, if I could just explain—"

"There's nothing to explain," Colonel Hanson interrupted sharply. "You were supposed to be home by five. It's now nearly quarter to seven. It's quite clear to me that our agreement is over."

Carole gasped. "But—"

"No buts!" Her father cut her off furiously. "I can't believe this. I thought I was doing a good thing by letting you ride again, by trusting you. But now I can see that I was a fool. I don't even know what to think of you anymore, Carole. I really don't."

Tears were running down Carole's face, but she hardly noticed. Why wouldn't her father let her explain? He wasn't even giving her a chance to tell him why she'd done it.

"What's going on in here?" a new voice broke in. Max strode through the partially open doors, glancing curiously from Carole to Colonel Hanson and back again.

"Sorry for the shouting, Max," Colonel Hanson

said. "But I've just come to pick up my daughter, who seems to think it's all right to be an hour and a half late for her curfew."

Max frowned. "I see." He stared at Carole. "And I understand your disappointment, Mitch."

"But Max!" Carole gulped, trying to keep her voice from shaking. "I was just trying to tell Dad that I—"

Max held up his hand. "Don't bother, Carole," he said. "You know how I feel. One mistake is one too many. That applies to this sort of thing as much as it does to riding or horse care. I'm very disappointed in you."

Carole's head was spinning. *Why can't they stop yelling for two seconds and listen to me?* she wondered in disbelief. *Neither of them even seems interested in hearing my side of the story!*

Just then the stable door creaked open again, just wide enough to admit Ben Marlow. He blinked at the little scene in the entryway in front of him, looking startled.

Carole stared at him for a moment as her father and Max continued to lecture about how irresponsible she was. So he had finally returned—far too late to save her, she realized with a sinking heart.

It's not like Ben is the type to step forward and offer detailed explanations, she thought bitterly, noticing that he wasn't even looking at her now. He was watching her father and Max, his expression as inscrutable as always. *He'll probably just sneak on past, and then I—*

"Excuse me," Ben said loudly.

Max and Colonel Hanson both glanced at him in surprise. It was obvious that neither of the men had noticed Ben's arrival. "Oh," Max said blankly. "Marlow. Er, what is it?"

Ben shrugged, seeming a bit surprised to have their attention. He stared at his feet, his voice now little more than a mumble. "Er, sounds like she's, uh—" He gestured at Carole. "I think I know what happened."

Max looked confused. "What are you talking about?"

"It's my fault." Ben cleared his throat, then looked directly at the two men. "I was late. She was covering for me."

Colonel Hanson frowned. "That's very noble of you, young man," he said, his voice stern. "But my daughter had a strict curfew, and she knew it. And I don't think—"

"Hang on a minute, Mitch." Max held up his hand. "Let's just hear what Ben has to say."

Carole held her breath. She stared at Ben, but he was still looking at her father and Max.

"I took some time off this afternoon." Ben shrugged again. "Uh, I had to—to take my niece to the doctor. Thought I'd be back in an hour. Told Red I would be back."

"You—Did you say your niece?" Max asked. From the expression on his face, Carole guessed that he'd had no idea what Ben's errand had been, or even that such a niece existed.

Ben nodded. "Sorry, Max," he said gruffly. "I let you down. Good thing Carole was here to pick up the slack."

Carole's mind boggled. She couldn't believe that Ben was sticking up for her. She'd never heard him speak so much in her life. *And I can't remember the last time I heard him say my name, either.*

The thought had just popped into her head, and she shook it out immediately. This wasn't the time for that.

"I'm really sorry, Dad," she said, taking advantage of the brief silence. "I took my curfew seriously, I really did. But Max was gone picking up Deborah, and Red was out on the trail, and the beginning riders needed help, and nobody else was here to take care of things, and I—I had to do it. I'm sorry, but I really didn't have any choice. I had to do it, even if it means getting grounded again." She stared at her father defiantly, realizing that it was true. "I think I made the right choice—the only choice. I'm sorry if you don't agree."

Her father was staring at her in astonishment. "Let me get this straight," he said, his voice less angry now. "There was no one here to take care of the stable. And this young man"—he waved toward

Ben—"this young man was supposed to return earlier—"

"Five o'clock," Ben put in quietly. "I should've been back by five. Latest."

Colonel Hanson nodded, though he hardly seemed to have heard him. "So you stayed to look after things here, even though you knew it meant breaking your curfew."

Carole shrugged. "I guess so," she said weakly. "I knew you'd be mad. But I told Red I'd stay until Ben got back, and I couldn't just leave. There was nobody else."

"I see." Colonel Hanson took a deep breath. "And I have just one thing to say."

"What is it?" Carole cringed, expecting the worst.

"I'm sorry, Carole." Her father stepped forward and put a hand on her shoulder, looking her directly in the eye. "You did the right thing. And I should have let you explain before flying off the handle."

Carole gasped. "You mean you're not going to . . ." She trailed off, unable to say the words.

"Ban you from the stable again?" Colonel Hanson's eyes crinkled slightly, though he didn't quite smile. "No, I don't think so. I'm starting to think that letting you ride again was the right thing for me to do. I wasn't so sure about that at first." He shrugged ruefully. "I suppose that's why I was so quick to jump down your throat when I thought you were flouting our new rules."

Carole could hardly believe her ears. "You mean I can still ride?"

"Four days a week," her father replied. "Just as we agreed."

Max smiled. "Sounds like a good decision to me," he said, patting Colonel Hanson on the back. "We kind of like having Carole around here, you know." He glanced at Carole. "By the way, I'm sorry, too," he said. "Looks like the mistake here was mine—not giving you a chance to explain."

"It's okay," Carole said, not quite believing that things were turning out so well after all. She shot Ben a grateful glance, still dumbfounded at the way he'd spoken up on her behalf. But before she could put her thanks for what he'd done into words, there was a clatter of hooves in the stable yard outside.

Max glanced at his watch. "Oops! Sounds like Red's back with his moonlight riders," he said. "Time to get to work."

"Yep," Ben said, already moving toward the door.

"Do you need Carole to stay and help out?" Colonel Hanson asked Max.

Max shook his head and smiled. "It's okay," he said. "We can handle it now. But thanks for the offer." He winked at Carole.

Colonel Hanson nodded and put his arm around Carole's shoulder. "All right, then we'll be going. I want to get started telling my daughter how proud I am of her."

Max and Ben had already rushed out to help Red, so they didn't hear Colonel Hanson's comment. But that didn't matter. As her father smiled proudly down at her, Carole knew that his words were meant for her.

FIFTEEN

"Extra! Extra! Read all about it!" Stevie shouted happily as she raced into the student locker room the next afternoon, waving a handful of copies of that day's Fenton Hall *Sentinel* above her head. "Hot new talent Stevie Lake makes the third page, wins Pulitzer Prize for her brilliant reporting!"

Callie looked up with a laugh, giving her boot one last yank. "I know, I know," she said with mock exasperation. "You're a genius. You've been telling me that all day."

Stevie grinned, glancing around the room. Most of her friends were there: Carole was straddling a bench, picking burrs out of a fleece saddlepad. Lisa was digging for something in her cubby. George Wheeler was leaning against the wall near Callie, absently tapping his riding crop against one leg. And Scott was lounging on the bench that ran in front of the wall of cubbyholes. Stevie felt herself blush slightly as she remembered her suspicions from the day before. But she didn't want to waste time worrying about that now. "Sure, maybe you're sick of my fame and fortune already, Callie," she said brightly. "But some of these guys probably haven't even read my amazingly insightful article yet." She tossed copies of the newspaper to Lisa and Carole.

"Wow, Stevie!" Carole exclaimed as she opened her copy. "You made the third page? That's pretty cool, especially since you weren't even sure they'd print your article at all."

Stevie shrugged modestly. "I know. It's not quite front-page, breaking headline news, but it'll have to do. For now, anyway."

"Well, I think it's great, Stevie," Scott said. "No matter what my sister says."

"Thanks." With effort, Stevie stopped herself from babbling at him. If Scott really did like her as more than a friend, that sort of thing wasn't going to change it. She would just have to keep a careful eye on him for a while and see what happened. "And guess what? Theresa was so pleased with the response so far that she said she might let me write something else next week. And not just the cafeteria menus, either. Isn't that cool?"

"Definitely," Lisa said.

Stevie glanced at her quickly. She'd already heard from both Lisa and Alex about the agreement they'd made to take a break from their relationship. It had come as a huge surprise, and she was still trying to take it in.

Meanwhile, Carole was scanning the article. "Wow," she commented. "This part's pretty harsh: 'It's clear to this reporter that certain people, Ms. diAngelo among them, just weren't prepared for the compromises and responsibilities of a truly adult relationship, at least judging by her behavior this week.'" She glanced up. "And that's only part of it. What did Veronica have to say about all this stuff you wrote about her?"

Stevie shrugged, not wanting thoughts of Veronica to spoil her big moment. She wasn't worried about her threats. What could she do to her, anyway? "Um, let's just say she wasn't too pleased," she mumbled.

Scott laughed. "That's the understatement of the century," he said. "She was practically spitting nails all day. I heard she even went to Miss Fenton to complain—about your article, and also about the whole marriage project."

"It's true," George said. "I was in the office when she came in."

"Really? So what did Miss Fenton say?" Stevie asked, wondering if Veronica's plans for revenge included trying to get Stevie expelled. That seemed pretty weak, even for her.

"I only heard a little," George explained. "Then they went back into Miss Fenton's private office. But the secretary told me that Miss Fenton already decided they probably won't try the project again next year."

"That's too bad," Stevie commented. Her gaze strayed back to Lisa. *All this love and romance stuff really is a lot more complicated than I thought at first,* she mused. *I mean, it's easy to predict some things about some relationships—like that Spike and I would be at each other's throats during this marriage project, or that Veronica and Zach would make each other miserable. But the real-life stuff? That's a little tougher. Who would've thought that Lisa and Alex would decide to break up? They say it's temporary, that they're still in love—but if that's true, why date other people? It just doesn't make sense.*

At the same moment, Callie was thinking about Stevie's article. *You know,* she told herself, sneaking a peek at George, who seemed determined to hang around the locker room as long as she did, *if someone read Stevie's article who didn't know any better, they might actually think that Corey and I were a couple. We came across as a perfect match.*

It was tempting to take that and run with it—maybe hint to George that there was more than just a silly assignment between her and Corey after all. That pretending to be married for a week had brought their true feelings for each other to the surface.

But she banished the idea as soon as it entered her head. *It wouldn't work,* she thought, leaning forward to retrieve her riding gloves out of her cubby. *Everyone, including George, knows that Corey already has a girlfriend. Besides, it would be the coward's way out. And I'm no coward.*

She realized that she'd been acting like one lately, though. And it had to stop.

"Hey, you guys," Lisa said, breaking Callie's concentration. "What are everybody's plans for this afternoon? How about a trail ride to celebrate the start of the weekend?"

"I wish I could," Carole said reluctantly. "But I really think I'd better stick around here today. I don't want to be even one second late getting home tonight. Not after yesterday."

Callie shot her a sympathetic glance. Before Stevie's entrance, Carole had been telling them about her near disastrous evening. Then Callie turned to Lisa and shook her head regretfully. "Not today," she said, thinking about all the trail training she wished she could do that day. "Scott and I need to head out in a little while, too. Dad wants us at some fund-raising thing tonight, and we've got to get ready. I'll be lucky to get in a half-hour session with Barq in the schooling ring." She couldn't help wishing, not for the first time, that she could just tell her father that she had better things to do than spend a perfectly good Friday night smiling blandly as some drunken senator or aide told dull stories about his latest junket to the Caribbean.

She sighed. If she was ever going to rebel, it certainly wasn't going to be today. She'd already set up a few appointments for that weekend to check out horse prospects. There was no way she was going to make her parents mad now.

Lisa looked disappointed. "Stevie? How about you?"

"Can't, sorry," Stevie said distractedly. She was flipping through the *Sentinel* again, her hair falling forward into her face. "Phil's meeting me here in a few minutes. He's taking me out to celebrate."

"Oh well." Lisa shrugged and sighed. "Maybe I should head home, anyway. I ought to check on Mom. . . ."

Callie noticed that Lisa didn't press George to come along on her proposed trail ride, and for once she was glad. As the others got up to leave, Callie glanced at him. "Hold on, George," she said. "Can I talk to you for a sec?"

"Sure!" he agreed, his face lighting up. "What is it, Callie?"

Callie glanced around. Stevie had already rushed out of the room, chatting excitedly with Carole. Lisa was pulling on her jacket near the door. The only one still seated was Scott.

Callie shot her brother a meaningful glance. Scott blinked, looking quickly at George. Then he gave her an almost imperceptible nod. "Heading to the parking lot, Lisa?" he asked smoothly, hopping to his feet. "I'll walk you out. I want to grab something to read while I wait for Callie to finish her ride."

Soon Callie and George had the room to themselves. Callie cleared her throat, gathering her thoughts. This time, she didn't want to leave any room for misinterpretation. "I want to explain something to you," she said carefully, standing up to face George directly. "It's about us being friends."

George shrugged, his smile a little uncertain now. "What? I thought we already talked about that."

"We did, but I'm not sure we covered everything," Callie said. "I can only keep on being friends with you if you can accept that that's all we'll ever be. Just friends. Nothing more." George opened his mouth to answer, but Callie continued before he could speak. "And I know you're going to say that you understand that, but I'm not sure you really do. That's why I think we need to take a break from our friendship for a while."

"What?" George protested, looking horrified. "What do you mean? We don't have to do anything drastic. I told you, I'm sorry for the way I acted the other day. What more do you want?"

Callie shrugged. "I'm sorry, George," she said firmly. "I just think this is for the best. I want us to keep our distance from each other for a while— maybe a couple of weeks. Then we'll see."

George grabbed her arm. "Come on, Callie," he pleaded. "We don't have to do this, really."

"Yes, I think we do." Callie could see that this wasn't going to be as easy as she'd hoped. She should have known that George wouldn't give in unless she forced the issue. "And to prove how serious I am about this, I think maybe I'd better leave Pine Hollow right now. I'm sure once you've had a chance to think about this, you'll see that it's the best way."

She turned and hurried from the room, half expecting George to follow. But he didn't. *Good,* she thought with relief, heading across the entryway toward the door. *Maybe that means he's finally catching on.*

With only a small pang of regret for the fact that now she wouldn't be able to train at all that day, Callie hurried across the stable yard to the parking lot. Her brother was there, leaning against the hood of his car, chatting with Lisa.

"Ready to go?" Callie asked briskly, already reaching for the passenger's side door. "We don't want to be late."

Scott looked startled, but he nodded. With a quick good-bye to Lisa, he hopped into the car and turned the key in the ignition.

Lisa felt a little forlorn as she watched Scott and Callie drive off. She sighed, fishing for her keys. *What now?* she wondered.

She didn't really feel like going home and sitting around watching her mother mope. But what else could she do? Her friends were all busy. She was all alone.

I guess I should get used to the feeling, she thought,

self-pity washing over her as she climbed into her car. *Feeling alone. Being alone. Without Alex.*

She sighed again, hating how weak and sad and pathetic she felt. Alex had become such a constant in her life that she really wasn't sure how to go about things without him. For the past year, no matter how confusing and complicated the rest of her life had been at times, he'd always been there, loving her, supporting her. And now she had banished him. Had it been the right decision? She still wasn't entirely sure. But she'd made the choice, and now she had to stick with it.

If we were meant to be together, we will be again someday, she reassured herself. *Someday soon. After all, what's one short month compared to a whole lifetime together?* She started her car engine. *Now all I have to do is figure out what to do with myself in the meantime.*

Carole had Starlight exercised, cooled down, groomed, and settled in his stall with fifteen minutes to spare. Glancing at her watch, she smiled and headed toward the student locker room, planning to leave a note in Rachel Hart's cubby so that the younger girl would know that Starlight was all hers for the whole weekend.

I'll miss him, Carole thought, shooting her horse one more wistful glance before turning the corner at the end of the aisle. *But at least now I know I can come back in just a few days.*

She still could hardly believe that things had worked out so well with her father. Not only was he still letting her ride four days a week, but he'd been so happy about how she'd taken responsibility for her actions the night before that he was talking about letting her start her job again, part-time at least, as soon as her probation was over.

Carole couldn't wait, though the idea of starting work again made her think about her intention to settle on a career path. She still wasn't much closer to making a real decision, although she'd managed to eliminate a few possibilities, like being a vet.

She was still musing about that when she looked up and saw Ben walking across the entryway toward her. It was the first time she'd seen him that day. "Uh, hi," she said, suddenly feeling awkward. She wanted to thank him for what he'd done the night before, but she wasn't sure how to do it without scaring him away as usual.

For a second she thought he was just going to nod at her and keep moving. But at the last possible moment, he stopped short and cleared his throat. "Hi," he said. "Uh, things okay? With your dad?"

"Yes." Carole smiled tentatively. "Thanks to you. I really appreciate what you did. You know, speaking up like that."

Ben shrugged as if it had been nothing. But then he coughed and shot her a sidelong glance, meeting her gaze momentarily before his eyes skittered away again and settled back on the ground in front of him. "I should be the one saying thanks," he said gruffly. "You know. The way you covered for me."

"Oh!" Carole smiled again. "No problem. I mean, you're welcome."

"No, really." Ben was still staring intently at his feet. His voice was so low that Carole had to lean forward a little to hear him. "I was late. If you hadn't been here . . . Well. Thanks. You know."

Carole shrugged, a little overwhelmed by the whole conversation. "Sure," she said. "You're welcome. But it was no big deal, really—I'm sure you couldn't help being late."

"Yeah." Ben shuffled his feet. "Well. My niece—you know. I have to . . ." He paused, as if struggling to find the words. "She doesn't really have anyone else. Just me."

Carole nodded. She knew she should probably just let it drop before she said too much and messed things up between them yet again. But her curiosity got the better of her. "How come?" she blurted out. "Er, I mean, your grandfather . . ."

"He's been sick." Ben didn't elaborate, just shrugged slightly. "And my sister . . . er, Zani's mother . . . Well. She's, you know, pretty much out of the picture."

This time Carole resisted the urge to press him for more details. She couldn't quite believe that he'd said so much already. "Oh. Okay."

"That's why . . . uh . . ." Ben bit his lip and glanced at her again, his dark eyes anxious. "You know. I've kind of been, well, acting sort of, er—"

At that moment the door of the indoor ring swung open and a crowd of chattering, laughing intermediate riders poured out, leading their horses. Carole winced, wishing she could turn back time and bar the door. Just when Ben had seemed to be on the verge of saying something important . . . maybe even something about that kiss . . .

But it was too late. With a mumbled farewell, Ben hurried off toward the tack room, leaving Carole standing alone in the swirl of activity as the younger riders streamed past her.

But despite the untimely interruption, she still couldn't help feeling optimistic about where things stood. *It wasn't exactly a full-fledged conversation or anything, like the kind two actual friends would have,* she thought, staring in the direction Ben had gone. *And maybe he still hasn't so much as acknowledged that kiss. Or a lot of other things.*

Suddenly remembering her curfew, she turned and headed across the entryway, dodging students and horses as she went. But she couldn't help pausing for one last glance behind her as she reached the door.

Still, it was something, she thought with a slight smile, picturing the way Ben's eyes had met hers, if only for a moment. *And maybe, just maybe, it's at least some kind of start.*

248

ABOUT THE AUTHOR

BONNIE BRYANT is the author of more than a hundred books about horses, including the Pine Hollow series, The Saddle Club series, The Saddle Club Super Editions, and the Pony Tails series. She has also written novels and movie novelizations under her married name, B. B. Hiller.

Ms. Bryant began writing The Saddle Club in 1986. Although she had done some riding before that, she intensified her studies then and found herself learning right along with her characters Stevie, Carole, and Lisa. She claims that they are all much better riders than she is.

Ms. Bryant was born and raised in New York City. She still lives there, in Greenwich Village, with her two sons.